the **826**
Quarterly

AN 826 VALENCIA ORIGINAL
Published May 2015
As the twenty–first edition of *the 826 Quarterly.*
Created by all hands on deck at 826 Valencia.

826 Valencia Street
San Francisco, California 94110
826valencia.org

EDITORS Molly Parent and Emma Peoples
EDITORIAL BOARD Alyssa Aninag, Pablo Baeza, Lauren Hall, Allyson Halpern, Desta Lissanu, Olivia White Lopez, Christina V. Perry, Amy Popovich, Claudia Sanchez, Ashley Varady
DESIGN DIRECTOR María Inés Montes
PRODUCTION COORDINATOR Amy Popovich
BOOK DESIGNER Tracy Liu
ILLUSTRATOR Eunice Moyle
COPY EDITOR Helaine Lasky Schweitzer

PLEASE VISIT:
The Pirate Supply Store at 826 Valencia
826valencia.org/store

ISBN 978-1-934750-58-2
Printed in Canada by Prolific Graphics
Distributed by Publishers Group West

the 826 Quarterly

VOLUME 21 ⁎ *Spring 2015*

⁎Published twice yearly, at least.

Contents

Waves Like Crocodiles: Non-Fiction

Jumbly, Gloriumptious: Excerpts

Now I Pose One Final Question: Journalism

At-Large Submissions

826 Valencia: Who We Are & What We Do

The Smooth Memories They Hold

E. EASTMAN * *Author*

On my bathroom counter lounges a squat, swanky glass bottle of an ambrosial amber liquid — *Giardino Veneziano nel Pomeriggio* I named it, or a "Venetian Garden in the Afternoon," a delectably intoxicating and heady scent redolent of the overheated bosoms of sixteenth century Venetian courtesans strolling walled gardens in towering, sophisticatedly-curled white wigs and splashy silk gowns, precious sparkling jewels encircling naked necks, lusciously intricate lace shawls draped from their shoulders like exquisitely exotic butterfly wings, the air abundantly aromatic of the burgeoning blossoms of fruit trees and spice-laden breezes. It is a scent concocted especially for me by Yosh Han, who is not only a practitioner of the olfactory arts but the original purveyor of pirate supplies in the emporium at 826 Valencia, a dear friend of the organization for over a dozen years, and, coincidentally, an apt recruiter—for when, four years ago, I found myself with time to spare, I presented myself to the enterprisingly intelligent folks behind the Writing Lab's palatial, burgundy velvet drapes.

Since then, I've tutored a plethora of kids through a plethora of projects, and had a front row seat to some pretty magical writing about which living person they most revere, the historical figure they most identify with, what they would come back as if they died, their most prized parties, what charities they'll donate to when they get rich and famous, disgusting things they've found in a refrigerator, traits they admire in themselves and those they deplore, their idea of perfect happiness, a time they have fallen, or been bitten, or bit, their greatest fears, their motto, what they would change about themselves if they could, what or who is or was the greatest love of their lives, when and where they were the most contented, what they love about themselves, what they'd like to improve, their dreams, their opinions, what confuses them, or angers them, how they express feelings, what feelings they hide, favorite memories, what has special meaning, things that were silly, things that were important, what they love to do, what they hate to do, things they miss, things they wish they had, what they could teach someone, what they would give the world, people they would like to meet, people they have met, people they miss, imaginary persons, their favorite place, the place they wish they could forget, dangerous places, safe places, what they want to be, what their parents want them to be, things they've lost, things they've found, home, a place visited often when younger, moments when they were very afraid, strange things people do, the best food they've ever tasted, someone who died, their first kiss, their last kiss, their first fight, their last fight, dogs, cats, iguanas, elephants, birds, mice, dirt, the worst things they've ever done, tractors, dancing, cooking, shopping, people who yell, people who whisper, shoes, things they need to throw away, favorite television programs, what they like most or least about summer, their prized funny stories, their guilty pleasures, cherished hobbies, treasured clothing, a bad hair day, their bodies, acne, allergies, their allowance, a handicap, siblings, or the times they've triumphed over adversity.

When I was eight years old I kissed every member of my Girl Scout group. Not once did I ever consider it being out of the ordinary, notes one of our contributors to this *Quarterly*.

I am a book that hasn't been written, avows another.

Their works demonstrate what good writing is all about: how we must straddle a saddle that rests between both sides of our brains, with the left, organizational, responsible for finding words and sentence structure and the intellectual delight to be discovered, to be procured, within the confines of dictionaries and thesauri; the right, associative, responsible for insight, attention, perception and orientation, visual imagery, the interpretation of context and tone, the making of rough estimations and comparisons, and the birthplace of metaphor.

What mastery, what word play, what an acute sensitivity to the sounds of language, to the rhythmical labial resonance of alliteration and of assonance at the back of the throat; the details—descriptive, noting a quirk of speech, a mannerism, the fashion in which hair falls across a face, a personal smell, the way a person walks, and lively verbs replacing adjectives and adverbs. Heed the tension, the tone, the point of view, how they differentiate truth from fiction, how they situate psychic distance, insert accurate dialogue, develop the narrative arc, how they underpin scenes with emotion, how they use themselves as characters, how indebted they are to emotional memory, to what the flesh remembers, to the limbic system, that group of deep brain structures common to all mammals, involved in motivation, behavior, olfaction, and emotion, inextricably entwining smell and memory, an inculcation of sensory details that can open up a story to readers, allowing them to enter a story rather than remain at a distance, as they do when the writing is more abstract.

It is, I believe, the key to good writing, to pushing it deeper, to manifesting meaning, to revealing the joy or sorrow beneath a descriptive surface: that if we can capture that singular smell of wax polish in that long-ago house, then other memories will swirl and tumble into existence. Details that can offer not only a way into the writing, but proffer a clue to its eventual shape. When I brought a vial of my venerated Giardino Veneziano to a workshop on journaling for pre-teens, and requested that each participant report on what image a whiff had contrived, one boy dashed off that it smelled like *the stuff my father sprays when someone has been in the bathroom too long.*

Within the ensuing *jumbly, gloriumptious* pages of this manuscript, then, I hope you'll be as ecstatically pleased as I am to find pizza smelling like *cheese, combo, pepperoni, cotton candy, and all the food and things in the universe,* water tasting like *fish and dirt,* waves that are like *crocodiles,* roses *red as fire,* cacti as *spiky as porcupines,* earrings as *shiny as the sun,* heels that sound like *cymbals,* cups of chamomile splashing down throats *like the smooth memories they hold,* lips lightly leafing like *two pieces of crisp paper trying not to crinkle,* and soufflés that, like love, if left with nothing but *time and a back turned to curdle in preheated silence under a soulless star, wilt like a blossom in the devil's hand.*

I say, plaudits to my peeps.

E. Eastman received an MFA in Writing from the University of San Francisco; his award-winning essays have appeared in the Noe Valley Voice, InDance, the Bellingham Review, Fourth Genre, and Switchback.

How does one tie a string around a whisper? Why is the sky blue? And how the heck did that boy get stuck in a glow stick? These are the questions that any writer of fiction must answer. Luckily, the writers collected here rise to the occasion, while leaving just a few mysterious stones unturned. You know, for suspense. Welcome to the land where snow monsters steal blue flowers, and their narrator invites us to enter the story: "It went like this..."

It Went Like This

Fiction

Why Is the Sky Blue?

GISELLE MALDONADO * *age 8*
Buena Vista Horace Mann

The sky is made with secret ingredients. It had to be made so everyone could breathe. After it was made, people threw blue glitter at it. Maybe it was a girl or a boy, or maybe a grown-up who was throwing blue glitter.

A crocodile was selling blue glitter every night. He was selling glitter so everyone could have it. He wanted everyone to have some glitter to throw into the sky. The sky could be turquoise or blue or sometimes even purple, when people threw glitter at it. Tell all the other people that they can throw glitter into the sky, too.

Anonymous Ancestor

CLÉO CHARPANTIER ✳ *age 16*
International High School

Beatrix had always wanted to fill the gap in her family tree—the hole where a great-grandfather should be, the chasm in the branches, the dark silhouette of an unknown ancestor. Her great-grandmother, whom she called Mémère, had mothered Beatrix's grandmother Claire when Mémère was sixteen, in the midst of World War II in occupied France. The father died shortly thereafter, before the war ended. Mémère later married a Frenchman who was a wonderful father to Claire and a loving great-grandfather to Beatrix. And yet, Claire never called him Dad, Papa, Père, or Father; and she never took his last name. But most importantly, she never asked about her birth father. No one ever did. The existence of her birth father was taboo in the household, and more so was his identity.

One day, after having been interrogated by her fourth-grade teacher on her last name and the fact that it didn't match her father's, Claire brought the question home to her mother and asked why. Mémère, with her apron on and greasy spoon in hand, broke down in tears, sobbed for hours, and was inconsolable for days. Claire never raised the subject in her presence again and neither did anyone else. But Claire remained fascinated by the mystery surrounding his existence. Although Beatrix's red hair and blue eyes were the tangible proof of inheritance, she also received an impalpable infatuation with the nameless great-grandfather. The unknown figure of her missing ancestor had loomed over Beatrix like a faceless ghost since her childhood. She decided to finally investigate.

At her great-grandmother's house for the weekend, Beatrix waited for Mémère to go up to bed after dinner before starting her ancestral search. Beatrix had struggled through two rounds of Boggle and a long round of Scrabble, losing pitifully at each, before her great-grandmother was ready to retire. After Mémère counted the points in her last word, *genealogy*, she yawned. Beatrix knew Mémère wouldn't bother to tally the total points because it was futile, but also because Mémère didn't want to embarrass her. Mémère put her tile racks back in the box and stood up.

"I'll go up to bed now if you don't mind," she said, her voice small and tired, running her fingers through her icy white hair. "I'll be up at six, but I'll try not to wake you. What will you want for breakfast? Do you have everything you need?"

Beatrix said she was fine and would take care of cleaning up the game, wanting to be rid of her as fast as possible to get on with the search.

She sat in the kitchen for an agonizingly long time, waiting for her great-grandmother to fall asleep. If he's German, that makes me half-German. If he's Jewish, that makes me half-Jewish. She tapped her fingers on the wax tablecloth covering the circular kitchen table, tracing the flowers with her pinky as she imagined a great-grandfather with Jewish features. He might have been a soldier or maybe a civilian. Maybe he was a hero or the enemy. She played with the Scrabble pieces left on the table, rearranging Mémère's last word in multiple ways. Genealogy, what a fitting last word for her to play. She imagined, she pictured, she dreamed up, she envisioned. A Jew, a Nazi, a hero, or an embarrassment. She conjured up several stories as she watched the hands of the clock tick by.

The forty-five minutes she waited felt like hours. She stood, then crept over to the dining room like a robber in a stranger's home, squinting against the darkness. It was darkness that felt like the manifestation of her lack of knowledge enveloping her life, caused by the chasm in the branches. Like a ballerina in the midst of a performance, she tiptoed to the closet—the holder of all secrets and answers—avoiding the floorboard that squeaked and might give her away. In it, her great-grandmother held all her memorabilia, her souvenirs, and her trinkets. The closet that night was a treasure chest holding gems hidden away for years, gems reflecting the face of her great-grandfather.

As she turned the knob and heard it click, she thought: *The hole will finally be filled, the chasm completed, the branch will regrow.* In the pale light, Beatrix saw all of Mémère's memories held in notebooks and pictures and letters and accumulated ephemera. She was certain there was a trace of her great-grandfather's identity somewhere among her things. Beatrix hoped to find a journal with the answer. Luckily for her, her great-grandmother had dated all her journals on their spines. Her excitement grew. 1946, 1945, 1945, 1944, 1943... "Here it is!" she whispered, grabbing the notebook and, in her haste, knocking the others over. She cursed under her breath as she put them back in their place.

She sat at the dining room table, holding the journal, looking at it, staring at it, examining it. The answers were right there, between her fingertips. Yet as she traced its spine with her index finger, she started to reconsider. In a sudden movement, she stood to return the journal to its place.

She didn't need to squint against the darkness anymore; her walk was certain and she wasn't stumbling through the obscurity. Her eyes had adjusted to the darkness, just like she had gotten used to the darkness left by the chasm in the branches. She had gotten so attached to her imaginary great-grandfather who was both German and Jewish, both civilian and soldier; she didn't want to be confined by one identity. She no longer craved proof of who he was, for the mystique had become more satisfying than the truth.

Zach Glows

DAVID CAMPOS * *age 7*
Thomas Edison Charter Academy

Zach is ten years old, and he is stuck in a glow stick. The glow stick has a mouth and eyes and can talk. Before he was in the glow stick, Zach had brown hair and brown eyes, but he drank the water inside the glow stick by accident because he could not breathe. One day, the glow stick broke and Zach fell out. He realized that the water had made him green. Then he looked in the mirror and saw his eyes had turned rainbow and his hair had turned green and purple.

The Desert

FERNANDA MERCADO ✳ *age 9*
Buena Vista Horace Mann

On September 19, there were three kids in the desert. Their names were Katy, Gael, and Ashly. Katy was eating ten cookies. The desert is a place where anyone or anything can die if you don't have enough water. If you bring water, you are super safe. If you bring 300 gallons of water, you are even safer.

This group was safe because they brought water. Their teacher, Lailoni, was super sleepy because they did a lot of walking and it was really hot. Her class was dying of thirst, but they had made a rule. The rule that they made was that they could only drink water on Fridays. It was barely Saturday, and they were already thirsty.

Gael said, "I am super hot. I am going to die if I don't have a glass of water."

Ashly said, "We are all dying, dummy!"

"You hurt my feelings," said Gael. Then Ashly pushed Gael. Gael started crying.

"I don't care if I pushed you and you got hurt. Don't be a cry baby," said Ashly.

Gael told the teacher. Lailoni said, "Don't push other people, or push anyone ever again." The teacher told them to drink water and gave them 100 cookies to eat. The kids were glad they had brought water to the desert. They learned not to push one another.

The Plans of Dofi

NAKAI CRISTERNA * *age 8*
Buena Vista Horace Mann

PART ONE

It was a stormy summer day in Brooklyn. This story is about a creature named Dofi, who is part dog and part fish. Dofi is a supervillain. He tries to kill all human beings. He can turn into a blowfish or a dog. He can shoot electricity out of his eyes and has a collar that lets him fly or swim. He hates human beings, because he thinks every being should be like him. He lives under the sea because there is land and water. If he wants to swim, he can swim, and if he wants to walk, he can walk.

His plan was to get tons of candy and lure all the children. Then the parents would come to try to get them, but they would be in the middle of the ocean.

Dofi got all of the candy in Brooklyn, and he tried to get all of the kids to follow him. But he only got a few of the teenagers. The teenagers finally caught up to him and they threw him in the ocean. They ate all of the candy and they got super fat.

PART TWO

Dofi had another plan. He got all of his water guns and all of his water tanks and all of his water slaves. Water slaves are part human and part water. Their shape is human, but they are made of water. They listen to Dofi because he is the Water King.

His plan was to turn Brooklyn into an ocean. The way that he was going to do that was to use all of his water guns, water tanks, and water slaves. First, he started to flood all of Brooklyn. He tried to do it, but Flame blocked his way. Flame is a superhero, and Dofi's enemy. Flame made a wall of flames, but Dofi's water tanks shot water and put out the flames.

But Flame didn't give up. Flame melted the water guns one by one, but it wasn't enough. Flame duplicated himself by ten. He destroyed all the guns, but the tanks were still there. The water tanks destroyed Flame. Dofi was sad that Flame was destroyed, so he brought Flame back.

He turned into a good creature in the end.

Fairies Live on Forest

ANDREA ALCANTARA * *age 8*
Thomas Edison Charter Academy

Fairies live in an icy place. They are not cold because they wear cozy clothes. They make ice cream. They eat all the flavors. Their favorite flavor is rainbow. It smells sugary.

The monster lives in a faraway castle. It is made of bones. It smells like dirty, rotten eggs.

There is a secret mermaid place. It is made by seashells. They are rainbow-colored.

The weather is very cold and icy. The sun is not too strong, so it is cold. There are icy mountains. The wind is icy. It can freeze you. The clouds rain down magical crystals.

War

JONATHAN RAMIREZ ✷ *age 9*
Saint James School

The weather is cold. The sky is as dark as a blueberry. There is no wind because the trees keep it out. It never rains. The people take baths, drink, kill fish, or wash their clothes in the beautiful river. There are clones that are protecting the people that live there. The clones have guns and armor, and the rebels are attacking them because they want to conquer their place. The rebels want to take their stuff, so they started a big war. The clones look like white statues, and the rebels are camouflaged.

Disoriented

JANELLE KUNG * *age 17*
Lowell High School

April's French beret and striped top stand out on the crowded, gum-covered sidewalks. Squiggly grooves form above her eyebrows as she squints, trying to orient herself in the foreign world of skyscrapers and flitting women and men in dark, official overcoats.

Pulling out her tattered map for the sixteen billionth time, April examines the lines that run off in nearly every direction possible. She wishes she knew this city like she knows her hometown, Paris. She runs her white-tipped, manicured nails along the creased paper, desperately hoping to find some point of reference. A small, pterodactyl sob escapes April's lipsticked mouth as she confirms again that she is completely lost. If only April could figure out where she is... but that, of course, is hopeless. There are too many roads, too many alleys, too many street names to go through. Not to mention, her English is worse than a two-year-old's. The only English words April remembers are hamburger and toilet, not too useful for her situation.

Tucking the map away in her skirt pocket, she continues her walk through the giant city. She moves away from the throngs of business people and turns. Her stilettos produce audible clicks that ring through the empty street.

As April wanders through the towering Financial District, she comes across a beautiful sight. Between two glossy high-rises, there is a view of a sparkling blue bay and a giant, fiery-red suspension bridge. She stops to admire the breathtaking view and then takes out her map again, hoping that the bridge will pinpoint her location. April's brown eyes scan the wrinkled paper, searching for the bridge. In a matter of seconds, she finds a bridge in the top right corner and a second bridge in the top left corner. Her eyebrows furrow. She realizes that the bridge is no help with finding her position. But if she guesses which bridge it is, and guesses correctly... no, better not risk it. April can just find a different reference point.

The skyscrapers taper out as she continues walking. They shrink into grand Victorian homes, marquee movie theaters, and small store fronts. It is as if April has been transported to a whole different city. She turns a corner to discover a busy intersection. It is bordered by various restaurants and a park crowded with red metal chairs.

The first thing April notices are the flags. They are striped with every color of the rainbow and are everywhere. They line the blocks in house windows, store windows, and even street poles. It is bizarre. All of the flags seem to have the same vivid design.

April is so absorbed by appealing bright flags that, for a second, she doesn't even notice that the plaza is flocked with men. No women. Just men, and they are all completely naked. It is strange because despite the fact that the men looked uniquely different, they all have the same carefree attitude of striding in their bare bodies. Embarrassed, April looks away to find something else to focus her attention on.

She scans her eyes down the block until they meet a dark huddled figure that she had not previously seen. It is a man of about April's father's age and he has a scruffy black beard and dreadlocks, which make him resemble an elderly Jack Sparrow. Captain Jack stands out from the other men for two reasons. One, he is not naked. He wears layers of ragged gray clothes that look like they have not been washed in months.

Second, Captain Jack does not seem to be doing anything at all. He sits alone, staring off into the street gutter, while everyone else is either in pairs or groups, chattering excitedly among themselves.

April figures he would be a good man to attempt to ask for directions because he has nothing to do anyway. She inches closer in her stilettos and a cardboard sign that was previously hidden by Captain Jack's leg comes into view. It is in English.

"Pluh-ease geeve me mun-ey," murmurs April, trying to phoneticize the foreign words.

"Do you speak French?" questions Captain Jack, in French.

"Excuse me, you also speak French?" exclaims April, as a wave of relief washes over her.

"Yeah, I'm from there. I noticed that we have the same accent," answers Captain Jack.

"Good. I'm from France, too. From Paris, and I'm taking a vacation here and I don't speak English. Everyone else does, and I'm lost. I'm scared. I can't figure out where I am. Where are we?" blurts out April.

"We are in the Castro," smiles Captain Jack. "Welcome to San Francisco."

Why?

SERGIO MAGANA ∗ *age 12*
Thomas Edison Charter Academy

Hello, my name is Shane the killer whale. Well, that's what you humans call me, because of what my ancestors have done in the past. I'm actually very nice, yeah, I'm the nicest out of my whole family. You humans see me as scary, and huge enough to hurt someone, but that's not what I want. If you guys don't believe that I'm nice, I've got proof.

One day I was just swimming, feeling the water gliding throughout my whole body, just minding my own business, until I saw a small, moving piece of wood. I swam up to see what it was, and as I swam more to see this moving piece of wood, it got bigger and bigger the more I swam. I saw three men flipping and swinging wooden paddles to make this piece of wood move. I heard one of the men shout out, "Hurry Jack, help us paddle the boat!" I thought to myself, *Hmmm, boat? Is that what they call the piece of wood?* Finally the boat flipped over; all the men sank in the water, but as soon as I swam up to save them they all swam away thinking that I would harm them. Once all the men saw me with a scared look, I swam away thinking, *Why? Why me? Why couldn't it be someone else that all the people are afraid of?* As I swam away, I felt something that I've never felt before: I felt something coming out of me. I blinked. After I blinked I saw a shining object. It was a pilot fish! The pilot fish whispered to me and said, "Hello

Shane, my name is Nicole. I'm here to help you. Let me tell you something: Shane, those people up there are only afraid of you because you're being yourself; you shouldn't worry about what those people think, you should only think about yourself." When Nicole told me that, it made me notice that she's right. I don't care about what those people think because I'm just being me.

Four years later

Now after all these years I've known Nicole, she showed me that I can be small, big, or even scary, but I can always have heart for who I am.

The Unicorns that Fell in S.F.

GIGI HENRIQUEZ ✳ *age 10*
Buena Vista Horace Mann

Once there was a land in the clouds named Unicorn-landia. In Unicorn-landia, there were three friends named Cupcake, Frosting, and Sprinkles. They got in a fight, but they made up because they knew something was coming.

The next day, thunder struck Unicorn-landia and the three friends fell out of the sky. The other unicorns were worried.

Frosting screamed, "Ahhhhhhhhhhh! We are going to fall near an orange, tall bridge, and I'm afraid of heights!"

Cupcake responded, "It's so obvious, Frosting, because you scream so loudly!"

They landed in a stadium where a baseball game was going on. Sprinkles said, "That was a rough landing!"

"No," said Cupcake, "that was awesome!"

"Okay, okay," said Sprinkles.

"I love the uniforms!" exclaimed Cupcake.

"Hey, I think I read a book about this place once. It's called San... San... San Francisco!" said Frosting.

"Oh yeah!" both Cupcake and Sprinkles said together.

"But we need to get back to Unicorn-landia!" said Frosting.

They all tried to use the teleportation spell, but landed in the San Francisco Zoo instead of Unicorn-landia! They decided to go inside, and they were impressed by all of the animals. They were happy until they saw the zookeeper.

"Uh-oh," said Sprinkles.

The zookeeper chased them with a net. The three unicorns kept running until they got to the beach. They were tired, so they decided to take a swim.

"Ahhhhhhhhh!" screamed two of the unicorns, because it was too cold.

"It's not that bad," said Frosting.

Even though they liked San Francisco, they used the power of friendship to get back to Unicorn-landia.

The Warmest Winter

FERNANDO GUTIERREZ ✳ *age 17*
Downtown High School

In Sequoia National Park, the cold winds of the winter evening grow more intense as the afternoon turns into dusk. The year 2029 is coming to an end, making treetops yellow and covering the grounds in snow and dead leaves. As trees mimic the wind, ice begins to fall from dark gray clouds. The sun begins to set, making it darker by the second. Felix the bobcat leaps out of his den. He stretches his two-foot-long body and straightens out his small tail. Stepping out of his home, he passes by a creek where water flows underneath a thin layer of ice on top. At this time of year, the water sources around Felix should be completely frozen and safe for animals to walk across. However, over the past thirty years, little snow has fallen and, when it does, the weather is not cold enough for it to stay frozen.

Hungry and cranky, Felix roams the open fields for a small mammal, hoping to make it his dinner. Quietly walking through the thinnest layer of white, half-inch thick snow, he places his snowshoe-like back paws into his front feet's prints, helping him move through the snow silently. Felix hears a group of squirrels under an orange-leafed oak tree with the help of extra tufts of fur on the ends of his ears that allow him to hear with accuracy. Felix begins to stalk the clueless squirrels. Slow and quiet, Felix moves alongside the bushes. He chooses his prey. Keeping his eyes on it, he creeps behind the farthest squirrel from the group. Pouncing on the defenseless animal, Felix immediately bites its neck with his long, sharp teeth, quickly killing it. As the rest of the group runs in different directions, Felix enjoys his fresh kill to start the very bizarre winter of his second year of life.

After he finishes his meal, Felix makes his way back to his den, satisfied. Bright stars that cover the sky shine through the tall trees covered in the thin layer of snow. Enjoying the stars, he listens to the river flowing clamly in the distance. Felix feels relaxed walking through the cold snow until suddenly he feels a sharp pain in his front paw. *Snap!* Felix has stepped on a trap. Realizing what he has gotten himself into, he panics. Trying his best to get out of the tight grip of the trap, Felix starts to bleed. Noticing the dark red snow underneath him, he stops trying to pull away. With so much blood lost, Felix begins to feel sick. He feels lightheaded, deciding to fall asleep so he can plan an escape with more energy.

Felix wakes up to the sound of something approaching him in the distance. He jumps up and looks around, noticing it is daylight. He turns to figure out what direction the noise is coming from. Felix begins to panic again as the crunching of snow begins to grow louder. Felix tries his best to calm down and stay quiet to make out the mysterious sound. Footsteps in the snow! They don't sound like the footsteps Felix is used to hearing; they sink into the snow deeper than an animal's would. As he lifts up his head from looking down at his icy paw, covered in dried blood, Felix notices an upright figure about forty feet away from him. It's a human! Felix has never come in contact with one. Nervous and scared, he stays put and thinks of a way to escape. He stands still as the unfamiliar species approaches him. He has a plan. Once the human releases Felix's paw from the trap, Felix will bite the human's wrist. When the human grabs onto his wrist with his other hand, Felix will make a run for it to the nearest den.

As the old, gray-haired man kneels over to open up the trap, Felix looks at his target. Felix removes his bloody paw from the rusty trap and bites the human's wrist immediately. Quickly grabbing his wrist, the man focuses on his hand and Felix takes the moment to run away. He limps as fast as he can to the nearest tree instead of running to his den, believing that it will be an easier place to hide from the man. Using his sharp retractable claws, Felix knows he can get up the tree swiftly. He leaps onto the tree, but is slowed down by the cut on his paw. Struggling to get up the tall oak tree, he finally reaches the top. He looks over at the hunter and spots him stepping into a vehicle. Felix notices cages stacked on top of each other in the back of the truck. He observes the cages carefully, realizing each one contains a bobcat inside it. He knows that if he can survive until the winter ends, then his paw will heal and hopefully he will be able to avoid the man with the cages. The loud engine of the truck, as the old man speeds off, brings Felix back to reality.

After the encounter with the hunter, Felix takes every step with caution. Using his gray-brown, spotted coat, he camouflages himself between bushes and in the grasses, emerging from the little bit of snow there is, trying to avoid contact with humans. As the weeks pass, Felix becomes more aware of the traps and the hunting. Avoiding them with ease, Felix notices one day that they have all disappeared. With that in mind, he realizes that winter had ended many weeks earlier than usual.

Over many years, the winters shrink even more. Winter now begins in late December and ends in late January. Bobcat hunting season gets shorter and shorter, because winter isn't lasting as long. With the seasons changing in a matter of one month, humans don't hunt bobcats as often. Felix and the rest of the well-adapted bobcats are catching on to this. They aren't bothered by the shorter winters, and are actually looking forward to their short duration. As long as shorter winters will keep the hunters away, climate change is of no concern to the bobcats.

Ode to Pizzaland

JASMIN GONZALEZ * *age 7*
Thomas Edison Charter Academy

Pizzaland is a planet. The whole planet and all the things there are made of pizza. My family can gobble pizza, then the pizza magically appears back. The pizza smells like cheese, combo, pepperoni, cotton candy, and all the food and things in the universe. Tree trunks are the crust, and the top is whatever kind! We are pizza when we go there. You can eat yourself. We can hear all the food transforming into pizza. When you hold it, it's warm like the sun. The pizza is all the colors in the whole universe. The crust is crunchy. It is greasy.

String Theory

KATE IIDA ✳ *age 17*
Drake High School

In the years following my brother Jamie's death, I sometimes left string in the street. It started out as a way to mark
the paths I had followed and the places I'd been. I bought myself
a spool of twine and brought it with me when I went looking
for images. I'd walk down the twisting streets of houses and
driveways filled with rusted 1950s Chevrolets and melted
plastic trolls with blue spiked hair and frozen expressions. I
started to tie my string around posts that led up the rickety
stairs that led up to houses with the doors banged in and the
shutters broken.

One winter night, when the fog in the breath turned to
icicles that hung like a braided beard from my red baubled
Christmas sweater with the reindeer on it, I went down the
rickety stairs with the cobwebs and spiders which leered with
their pincers in the darkness. Clomp, clomp, clomp, down
the staircase to the basement where the damp and the mold
combined to make a stew: a softly simmering cauldron of
appearances and deception.

I stopped by mailboxes covered in markings in a language
I knew was spoken by the insecure. I climbed hills covered in
mud after a thick springtime rainstorm. I tied string around
wet, soggy boxes that had once been packages but were lost now.

In the damp and musty boxes that lay like orphaned children making imprints in the dust, I found what I was looking for: a pair of white boots with blades so sharp they made my fingers turn red with bits of rubies and stinging nettle.

At the bottoms of these hills, I climbed down into the creek beds where the water slipped mistily over piles of polished stones and the stinging nettle thorns scratched my face and arms. In these creek beds, adventure and a desire for thoughts made me tie strings around the bridges that held up the driveways where husbands came home to dinner late and tired and angry for reasons they were too afraid to think of, as pots and pans hanging from the walls crashed to the floor.

On the way up the steps I kept the hallway dark and the footsteps soft, but the door with the screen on it couldn't be made to keep quiet and banged like a pot falling from the stove on the front door.

I tied my string around whispers that I heard when I was outside late at night, alone on the front porch beside the tomato plants.

And before I could run or even hide, there was a cracking from the staircase and a whispered, "shhh," and then a creeping around towards the side where there was no window and then my brother, Jamie, with his brown curls flopping and his hair tousled because of sleep and his sweater so large it fell over his hands looked at me and asked, "What are you doing?" And to say something I held out the ice skates and my eyes went large and my feet went cold because of the thought of not being able to go. But my brother Jamie held out his thick, browned hand, which smelled like pine needles.

I waited until my hair smelled of pine needles. Then I went back inside with my string.

Then there was the time I went to the beach in the moonlight, which reflected off the water, and confused my eyes into thinking seagulls were as inconsistent as shadows.

And in a moment we were skidding in the rough moonlight and the pine trees beside us stood tall like sentries at the gates of belief. And in the light of a full-blooded, inky moon our feet crunched through the snow until we reached the place where the water turned to glass, like a reflecting mirror, and beneath the surface the fish glowed red, orange, and purple, and their eyes burned like coals in a fire pit.

On that night at the beach, we brought out candles and we held them together in the center of the circle and let the light reflect off them like coals in a bonfire. We stayed there, shivering, because we thought the light would keep us warm. I brought out my string and tied it around the candles and the circle, and saved it for the times of darkness.

I tied my string around the big, black, leather boots I wore for explorations.

As I began to lace up the skates, my brother Jamie took his big black leather boots and stepped on the glassy mirror-ice. Five steps forward, two steps back, side, side, back again—twice.

I kept the string as I took step after step down the long unpaved street.

"I think it's alright," he said, and the silver blades glistened until they slid onto the ice.

I tied my string around my lamp, which I kept beside my bed. But although I held it there longer and longer, I couldn't keep the light from going out.

There was a crack like the pan hitting the floor but louder, and the glass shook and I fell backwards on a piece of snow-drift and my eyes flew in circles until the lights went out like a match blown. Another bit of light lost.

And then there was the day I ended up in the freight yard, where the trains come in with their coal deliveries— I tied my string on one of the nails that stuck out of the side, so my string could see the world even though I was stuck at home.

In the freight yard I saw him— with a brown beret cocked sideways, digging in the dirt with a nail that stretched larger than his hands and so deep into the ground it seemed it could wrap twice around the world before coming back up again.

When I saw his nail, I thought of a giant system of nails that would intertwine like roots down into the core of the earth and they'd hold all the continents together in their iron fists. Seeing that, I knew I wanted to tie a string around them, to keep this image forever in the back of my mind as a memory of connection. So I climbed down by the side of the train tracks and lay down on my stomach and slid down into a small clearing of trees. I lay by the side of a rock beneath the green canopy of a redwood tree and watched. In my mind I took one end of the string and began to weave it throughout the picture—across his hat, down his arm, to his wrist, through the nail, and back again. Then I started on the other string, because I wanted to tie it together, like a package left out on the doorstep in a cardboard box in the middle of a rainstorm, the kind that turns dark brown and squishy-soggy and smells like moldy, paperback books when it is brought inside the next day.

But before I could complete the knot a train came rattling by, full of steam and rusted iron and the screeching of metal on metal, and he jumped up. He dropped his rusted nail on the broken shards of grey-brown slate rock beside the track and ran down, past the yard full of abandoned freight cars, to a place where I could not see him anymore.

My brother Jamie went to live with the multicolored fishes for so long that he forgot how to live without them. So the multicolored fishes brought him deeper, closer, so that he reached near the bottom so his glass eyes could deal with the darkness beneath the ice.

And the multicolored fishes kept leading him lower and lower down, until he forgot which way was up. That's what happened to my brother. Maybe someday he'll remember. Maybe someday...

I lost him like I lost my brother Jamie, like the thick brown hand that clawed at the edge of the ice before sinking down. I let the multicolored fishes take him because I was afraid of the cold and because I thought it was a game, that there'd be a second chance, that maybe he was just hiding beneath the surface for a chance to explore the underside of ice. I didn't realize that there would be no second chance until it was gone.

Suddenly, I feel a crunch to my side. I roll over and look up. He stands next to me, wordlessly, quietly, extending a thick brown hand. It smells like pine needles. When I feel for the string next to me, it's gone.

The Amazing Creations of Connie

ODALIS ALVAREZ * *age 9*
Buena Vista Horace Mann

One day, a little girl went to the library and saw a book that caught her eye. It was called *The Amazing Creations of Connie*. She picked it up and saw that this book was magical. It looked like one of the characters was running! He was a big, white, snow monster who looked like a marshmallow. She started reading the story. It was about a girl named Connie. It went like this:

One day, the villain was flying and he turned the sky black. Connie was flying. She fell because of the smoke. Connie fell into the ground and her bones cracked and her leg hurt a lot. The villain left and flew away. Connie screamed, "Ouch!"

Connie was on crutches and said, "I want to heal myself." Luckily, her superpower was healing broken bones.

Connie went on an adventure to meet the villain. She went to the mountains to get blue flowers. There was no snow monster in the mountains when Connie got there.

Connie pulled the blue flowers. The snow monster came behind Connie and she ran. Connie tripped, but luckily, her leg was better. The snow monster took the blue flowers and kept them forever.

Connie thought the sky would stay black forever. She went to sleep and had a dream about how to turn the sky blue again. She didn't have blue flowers, but she could use blueberries! She smashed blueberries and threw them into the sky. The sky turned blue again!

Poetry can be hard. It's not easy to imagine being a balloon tied to a chair, when all you want is a Mexican hat. Poetry is complex. Do you know the rules for writing a sestina?! Go look it up. We'll wait.

But the beauty of poetry is that using few words to express big ideas always results in something bold. Phrases like *saccharine dust*; a *blossom in the devil's hand*; a *cactus two blocks away as spiky as a porcupine. Frank Sinatra with a cold.* Read enough of these poems, and it all looks easy. It all seems simple. We all feel bold.

Easy, Simple, Bold

Poetry

Love Carries On

RUBY KLEIN * *age 14*
The College Preparatory School

My mother's hands are fragile,
brushing against a cool and delicate teacup
as she passes you the milk, watchfully.
Sunday afternoons with cups of chamomile,
splashing down our throats like the smooth memories they
    hold.
Touching her chilled hand,
knowing strength is embedded in the lines that make skin
    weathered and weak.
Intricate designs on the cups,
but I always chose the plain blue one,
because I wanted to sip these moments with attention to the
    detail
of her voice and her fingers picking apart her sandwich,
layers of experience she was spilling into my mouth.
Love didn't have to be designed with vines and flowers
growing over each other,
competing for room,
love carried on as simple as the pastel blue china
in front of me.

My father's hands are powerful,
controlling the room with a wash of his arm,
making me feel safe and captured with a flick of his hand.
My hand wraps around the ripples in his fingers.
His whole hand can devour mine,
as I grab onto him so tightly his hand blushes at my
    excitement.
He can silence the room from the control of his fingertips,
his power is in his presence,
shooting out of his words, his eyes, his movements.
His aura is persuasive,
as if hands could make people feel something,
as if they could change people's minds,
as if hands could change the world.
The crevices between his fingers
could captivate and convince any room
of the importance of his words.
My mother's hands are gentle.
Thin waves pass over them,
leaving them refreshed and lightweight.
My father's hands are tough,
feeling the sandy, scratchy surface of a bag of sugar,
collapsing into softness when you squeeze it.
My mother's hands are emotional.
Her steady hands become hot when she boils over,
from too much hot water in my grandmother's teapot,
her heavy clenched fist could cause a tsunami.
My father's hands are stable.
Anger cannot travel to his fingertips,
his shaking hands only know low tide.
My mother's hands are cautious.
Careful strokes are all she can paint,
her clarity can be muddled with a drop of milk.
My father's hands are daring.
Wavy movements and wave-inducing ideas,
he needs rough exfoliants to reach the raw of his fingertips.

And my hands are made of their fingers intertwined,
a recipe of ebbing emotions
sometimes cool to the touch
and sometimes hot enough to burn the roof of your mouth.
Sometimes I rummage the shore, destroying the beach
and sometimes I spill over lightly like a calm tide.
My hands are hers,
my hands are his,
my hands are mine.

My Life

TEODORO KIMBAL-DIRECTO ✳ *age 8*
Buena Vista Horace Mann

I am from fog in the morning,
and roses as red as fire.
I am from trees as green as a witch.
I am from a car-fixing shop next door,
also from crossing the leafy neighborhood.
I am from my mom rushing me in the morning.
I am from a cactus two blocks away that is as spiky as a
    porcupine.
I am from a dad who takes me to San Jose every Christmas,
also, a dad who tells me to never give up.
I am from jalapeño bagels and Mexico.
I am from my favorite ice cream, grasshopper pie.
I am a branch from my family tree.

If I Was a Balloon

JASON CAZAREZ * *age 9*
Marshall Elementary School

If I was a balloon I would be worried,
because I might pop or maybe I might pop myself.
But I would forget about it because I would have fun these
    days.
Like getting tied to a chair, that would be fun,
because you could spy on people.
And I would have more experiences, like visiting places,
like Mexico, Texas, Los Angeles, Las Vegas, and would have
    more fun—
by buying stuff like a Mexican hat.

Thin Man

EMILY GORDIS * *age 17*
Homeschooled

The bath water's a little bit blue.
I can't tell if it's from my hair
or from my heart, which sings the blues
like Frank Sinatra with a cold.

On Sunday morning
I read the news in bed,
and in the frozen food aisle,
I lived through an arctic winter.

Ice animals took shape because no one
knows how to close a door around here
where children press their faces up to the glass
and pretend winter comes to California.

The linoleum floor took on the aspect of Eden
and I waited by the ice cream and frozen hospital dinners
for free food samples,
or enlightenment.

On Sunday evening, I read all night and
babbled in the morning about the Minotaur
and minor gods,
like minor wounds.

Morpheus died a hundred years ago
and left legions of insomniacs with an atomic bomb
and no idea what love meant
while their cities burned in mushroom clouds.

If I say I've spent too much time waiting at SFO
it's only because those hours stretch long in my memory,
proving that time isn't linear
like liars and bankers say,

and planes never land on time,
so I'll listen to pirate radio coming out of the desert
and watch the domino row
of twenty-first century faces.

From up here we can see the Christmas lights.
He gives me earplugs, and never calls me back.

My Passion

ABIGAIL GIRON ✶ *age 8*
Alvarado Elementary School

I started at five, and I am eight now.
Look, look at that now—that's a talent!
Do you think sing, sing is my passion?
I cannot dance. You might laugh.
I cannot rap. You might laugh,
but I am eight,
and I want my passion to last.

How Is Love Like a Soufflé?

COSIMO COMITO-STELLAR * *age 16*
Lowell High School

They rise like the sun
when monitored with tender care,
and shine like the moon
with saccharine dust.
Molded from batter
sickeningly sweet or surprisingly savory,
they are stirred to perfection
when stark peaks
are forced to fold.
But,
if left with nothing but
time and a back turned,
to curdle in preheated silence
under a soulless star,
they wilt like a blossom
in the devil's hand.

A Fish

NOE CAMPOS * *age 8*
Thomas Edison Charter Academy

I see fish in the river.
If I was a fish,
I would look
for food like crumbs.
I would feel happy.
I would be
shiny and blue.
I would be
medium
size.
I would have a fish family
and it would be
my dad
and my mom
and brothers.

The Place You Left Me

NAOMI SMITH * *age 15*
Newark Memorial High School

I said it, please don't forget it.
I built up enough courage,
so why is it that you think it's something I'll regret?
I identify with the men
who chopped off their sex organs
and taped them on their chest,
because being black and male in this world
was just too difficult.
I identify with the little girl who puts on basketball shorts
instead of a dress for her seventh birthday,
while her mother hibernates in the kitchen,
praying to all the gods that her little girl isn't gay,
that this is just a phase that'll pass like the seasons.
My life provider
thinks he's my decider.
He talks about what society will do to me,
as if I'm a box of recalled produce.
I wish he'd understand my desire in life

isn't to have mass appeal,
but self thrill.
To have an identity and to identify are two different things.
Identity is an opinionated perspective given to you at birth,
by society;
to identify is a self-driven action.

Yes Mom, Pop,
I identify with lesbian.
This does not mean—I'll be a strung out freak
in a Motel 6.
This does not mean I'm not
human.
Please understand—
I've walked in places where trouble was me,
I've roamed in spaces where there was no light.
You can read my future off my palm,
beat me with sticks
till my skin turns purple and blue,
but never will I ever walk backwards into the place
you left me.

Night

RONALDO RODRIGUEZ * *age 10*
Rooftop Elementary School

School no longer lives—
no homework at all, no school.
I'm cozy in bed.
Night, peaceful, darkness,
stars shining bright like the sun.
No one to be seen.

Christmas

IRIS MORRELL * *age 15*
The Nueva School

Christmases in America are not who I am,
but I am also not *Glockenspiel* or *Lebkuchen*.
I am bloodline of an immigrant,
but my words are not defined by my culture.

I am rubbery cakes, homely delicacies made wrong.
I am illegitimate sons, little red books, powdered sugar,
    vanilla *Kipferln*.
I am the need to italicize, because I am a new language.

I am the shovel used to bury the family I never met.

But who would ever know?
Because my culture is an out-of-use currency.
If you came on a boat you might have seen foam crash
    against the stern,
but I am the generation lost at sea.

But I am not a tradeoff.
I am not an option.

I am, when you must leave or you must die, what lies beyond
the horizon.
I am decades beyond ballots, safe spots, being scared when
you cross the street.
If I wear a star on my chest, it is because I am proud.
You can never know what I will be.

I am not a Jew.
I am gray, I am light, I am many degrees removed from
Schwarz.
I am a changed name, a new place, forgotten friends, I was
raised to be not Jewish.
I have inherited a rejection,
intentional.
I am bribed sailors, blind Nazis, stamped postcards,
I am American.
I am free-thinking, book-reading, poem-writing,
because, on Christmas and in America, I know I can be.

Future Me

ERIKSON MARTINEZ ✻ *age 13*
Buena Vista Horace Mann

Do not get bored in school,
help people because some people need our help,
go to a good college,
learn more and pay attention,
help your family,
don't get in trouble,
be an engineer and make buildings,
have fun.
Play soccer.

My Sparkly Dress

KEILY PONCE * *age 8*
Moscone Elementary School

My favorite dress is super sparkly, pink, and longer in length.
I wear it with the earrings as shiny as a sun,
     sparkly bracelet, white heels, and ruffle socks.
My heels sound like a cymbal.
I wear a soft crop sweater (a black one) and a white purse
     with pearls,
and a white, sparkly hair bow.
The hair bow is white like my grandpa's cat.

Joint Aura

ZORA ROSENBERG * *age 17*
Lowell High School

You have a competitive air (or aura?)
about you, you seem loud and bold.
You make socializing seem so easy.
That might have been why it was so easy
to develop some kind of affection for you, if I had an aura
it would involve a message in bold
font saying, "**talk to me**." But it'd be too small and not bold
enough, and it's not easy
for me to socialize, and I can't do anything like aura
reading. But if we had a joint aura, I hope it would be easy,
simple, bold.

Two names that mean one person. That's how one writer in this section sums up her identity. In fact, all of the pieces of non-fiction writing collected here address the "other" side of their writers; they deal with memories, accumulated experience, first kisses, and all the parts of these young authors that you can't see on the surface. And what varied stories lie beneath: one of them is an optimistic blast of rainbow! At least one of them can swim! We're honored to be invited in.

Waves Like Crocodiles

Non-Fiction

My Name and Me

MAY WANG * *age 15*
Albany High School

In Chinese, family names come before given names. In Taiwan, my last name, Wang, is like the last name Smith in the United States and, to me, it's a blanket that wraps my family together, a reminder of all the things we have in common. When people say my full Chinese name, "Wang Rae Hsuan," the *Rae* comes out sharp and to the point, while *Hsuan* slips out softly, like caramel I roll around my tongue. Two sounds that are completely different and yet connected, like the two sides of me: the practical, straightforward person who folds her clothes in neat rectangles, plans, and stresses over everything in her life, and the girl who wants to let everything go and do something crazy.

My parents didn't come up with my Chinese name until I was three days old. Until then, my family called me *mei mei*, which means "little sister" in Chinese. That was how, two years later, when I moved to America, my mom connected my identity in my family with May, a word that in English means the fifth month of the year, a month that doesn't really have anything to do with me. It's like my mom tried to fit together two puzzle pieces—two cultures that don't really go together. *May.* When people say it, I think of a block thudding on wood—a dull sound. Yet, over the years, it's a word that has come to represent me.

Two names that mean one person. Sometimes I dream of going to a new city, getting a new name, shedding May Wang and Wang Rae Hsuan, with all their burdens, like a snake sheds its skin. I want to taste the freedom of becoming a new person in a place where no one knows me, but I know deep down that I won't. I'll always be May Wang and Wang Rae Hsuan. Those two names will always mean me.

Well, There Was No Tongue Dancing

MARIA RIVERA * *age 16*
Immaculate Conception Academy

The message was clear when my eyes met his. It was happening. Today. It seemed like such an established event, I felt it was almost appropriate to put it on my calendar with a date, time, and location.

I hadn't seen him since our eighth grade graduation. A short boy with a mop of curly, black hair awkwardly placed on his head, the most vivid memory I have of him is when we were in the sixth grade. We were on our outdoor education trip and, for no reason at all, he rammed me into the small creek we were exploring. Now here he is, five years later, participating in the same web design internship I was so hesitant to apply to. I almost didn't recognize him the first day we were in the office together. He looked different, taller, with sharper facial features. Puberty had been good to him, I thought. He definitely had better manners. But what surprised me the most was that out of all the people I wanted to lay one on me, he made his way from being one of the last to one of the first.

I stole glances at him from behind the gigantic screen of my monitor, careful not to make eye contact a second time. That would look needy. But at the same time, all I wanted to do was look into those gorgeous brown eyes—like God had made his irises out of honey and added in small flecks of gold. He had those cute lips, the kind that male models often have to have photoshopped on their faces, the kind most girls consider "kissable," the kind I'm going to...

I was pulled out of my girlish daydream by a sharp chime coming from the main monitor. Five thirty. Oh God, this is it. This is real life. It's happening. I quickly packed up my things, making sure I wasn't leaving anything behind because there would be no time to come back.

I silently slipped away from the office and half walking, half running, made my way to the farthest staircase, the only one that had a small platform with a single window that gave a peeking view of the neighboring building's roof garden. And then I just stood there. Waiting. Anticipating. Worrying. What if I'm a horrible kisser? What do I do with my hands? Oh God, what if my hair gets in his mouth? Maybe I should put my hair in a ponytail. But ponytails aren't sexy. Yeah, no, that's a no-go on the ponytail.

I stood there for what seemed like hours, palms sweaty, heart pounding. Pounding way too fast, actually. I was almost sure my heart was thudding the number of beats per minute that indicates when a person is about to go into cardiac arrest. Come on, where was he? I checked my phone. 5:34 p.m.

"It's only been four minutes," I growled at myself, "get a grip."

I waited another two. Maybe I had gotten the wrong message. Maybe this wasn't going to happen today. Maybe this wasn't going to happen at all. It could have been that he'd just glanced at me. I mean, we were friends. What if I'd just made a complete fool of myself?

I heard the gentle *pah-dha, pah-dha* of his sneakers getting progressively louder as he walked from the hallway into the corridor of the staircase. He smiled, those supermodel lips curving up, creating small dimples. He came up to me, totally confident, and just stared directly into my eyes. In that moment, I could have sworn that the walls just melted away. There was absolutely no sound and the world was spinning. He opened his mouth as if to ask me a question, closed it, slightly parted his lips again, and leaned in. That's my cue, I thought, and we closed our eyes, those beautiful brown eyes disappearing in a black cloak of darkness.

His lips lightly leafed against mine, like two pieces of crisp paper trying not to crinkle. His mouth was dry and he kept twisting his head in such an exaggerated left and right motion I was scared his neck was going to break. Instead of meshing, our lips were pulling at the ends and chafing painfully. I thought maybe I was just leaning too far back, so I tried to lean forward and as I did his teeth kept clashing with mine as if they were the locked gates of a golden city I was forbidden to enter. Maybe this kiss was like a concert: you have to get through the opening act before you can enjoy the main event. So I waited, trying to mend the broken rhythm of our bodies with my arms around his neck, his arms by his side. And then it finally hit me: this was the main event. This is what I had waited in line for—a sold out show where we find that the only performer sounds better on a CD than he does live. As quickly as it had started, it was over. He stopped and I opened my eyes to see him smirking back at me.

"I hope that makes up for the shove in the river. See you around."

With a quick wink, he walked away with the strut of a champion.

Um, wait, what? That was it? That was the big kiss that I had been anticipating since watching *Titanic*? Was this a joke? Please tell me this was a joke. Nope, he was gone. That was really it. Was that satisfying for him? Did he really believe that I was going to be impressed by the awkward clamoring of teeth or that horrible feeling of dry lips scraping against my own? Walking away, he gave the impression that he'd just given me the best possible first kiss a human being could possibly give to another. I felt a little embarrassed for him, that he could be so painfully wrong.

Some books give you all this descriptive detail about magical kisses: their tongues danced, his lips crashed onto hers, she heard fireworks going off in her head. All these beautiful, passionate scenes of these kisses that somehow have become this stereotypical and symbolic rite of passage into womanhood. Well, there was no tongue dancing. I don't know how there were going to be crashing lips if there were hardly any lips to begin with. Like, they were only on his face for the purpose of decoration. There most definitely weren't any sparks. I felt like I was burning in a forest fire when I was waiting by myself, in the moment leading up to the kiss. The kiss, if you can even call it one, was like a rainstorm that completely extinguished every single flame, not even leaving a tiny little ember that survived.

Muslimah

HANA ABDULLA * *age 16*
John O'Connell High School

I was in the first grade when I decided I didn't want to go to school anymore. I can't remember how or where, just that I didn't want to be in another class and face those mean little girls again. I was six and it was the fight-or-flight instinct people say comes naturally. My body was begging me to fly. All I remember is being scared, humiliated, and upset. I didn't have the words to say what I wanted, and even if did, I didn't trust that those girls would be any less ignorant. My eyes were closed and as I tried to keep my head up and swallowed back tears, those two little girls said things like, "You can't play with us because you're a terrorist." They laughed as I stood there, realizing that this would be a title I would have to deal with for a very long time.

Being a Muslim American made things really difficult in school because I always felt uncomfortable. Growing up, I was always taught never to hit anyone or speak if I had nothing nice to say. So I stood there, me against them, feeling helpless. I no longer looked forward to another day of school.

After I moved into my second year of first grade, I became successful. Because I bantered my way out of further conflicts, I had failed first grade. During my second year, I was selfish and inconsiderate and gave my parents a hard time so I could avoid as many school days as I could. I hid in my closet on mornings leading up to school, the trunk on my arrival to school, and toy structures or in the reading hall during our free play. Despite my resistance, the second year was better and I finished at the top of my class. I never said a word to anyone about what had happened. I would like to believe I am stronger now than when I was six and that my experiences made me stronger, but I think I just became used to it.

Growing up as an Arab Muslim in America taught me to admire both cultures. I always thought of them as equals. As I grew older, I cherished my Arab side more because I found it to be an important part of who I am and what I love. It was, however, something easy to lose while growing up in a Western society my whole life. It helped to have such a liberal family. My family is very liberal, which just means that they are open to new things. Although we maintained our traditional language, food, hospitality, and music, we also incorporated many American things, like conforming to the Western way of dressing and celebrating such holidays as Thanksgiving and the Fourth of July.

We were just normal people doing normal things. Anyone who knows us understands the type of good-hearted people we strive to be. But it was the constant casualties of walking down the street or going to the mall with relatives who wore the hijab that I found difficult to endure. Simple things always seemed to involve some type of stereotypical interaction. Some days, it would be simple and we'd get the usual "Terrorist blah blah blah get out of my country blah blah blah," or the hilarious "Helllooo it is ve-ry niiice to meeett youu," which stretched out every syllable two seconds too long. To this, we would reply in fluent English, "You, too," slightly questioning whether it really was nice to meet them. I always tried to hide my dirty looks or condescending smile when they appeared dumbstruck. People sometimes assume that if you wear the hijab, you aren't educated, aren't from here, or don't speak English. Other days, it was worse. The physical incidents were the most terrifying. I always heard of the things other people encountered, but I always hoped it was exaggerated.

Fast forward to fourth grade. I had been living in Daly City for almost two years and was visiting my family in San Francisco. One day my sister, three of my cousins, my aunt, and I were on our way back from Safeway. We were crossing the street and waiting for my aunty on the opposite side of the crosswalk when a red truck came rushing around the corner. Two white men shouted dirty racial slurs and threatened to hit my aunt and her baby lying unaware in the stroller. I was silent and everything seemed to go mute. She sped down the pedestrian walk, running for her life. It was really frightening and painful for her children and me to endure.

Now listen. I am not saying that all Arab Muslims are saints. There is some truth to the stereotype, as each one originates from some small truth. A few people who identify themselves as Arab Muslim have done totally unjustifiable things. In reality, none of what they claim to be Islamic is true and their actions are, in fact, blasphemous. Muslims all over the world condemn these actions and stand together to try and stop the stereotype. As *the Daily Beast* states:

> "And once again with ISIS, we have seen universal condemnation by Muslim leaders in the United States and abroad. For example, the two biggest Muslim-American groups, ISNA and CAIR, unequivocally denounced ISIS. CAIR's statement notes in part: 'American Muslims view the actions of ISIS as un-Islamic and morally repugnant. No religion condones the murder of civilians, the beheading of religious scholars or the desecration of houses of worship.'"

Muslim people around the world are constantly standing up and proving themselves to be peaceful people. We are trying to reach past the blinding labels on the television screens and newspapers to show the world the true representation of who we are, rather than the negative things they've heard.

Even though being an Arab Muslim American can sometimes put me in uncomfortable situations with others, I will never let their opinion sway mine. I know who I am and I do not need a bunch of ignorant people to tell me otherwise. I know what my people are like and that each person is different in their own way. I know that being an Arab Muslim American means that I am supposed to represent peace and acceptance, and I will strive my whole life to do so. I will continue to be who I am in hopes that one day, the perception of my people will change. But for now, knowing who I am and being strong enough to stand by it are enough for me.

Debris

MELANIE HARRA * *age 16*
John O'Connell High School

It was the absolute epitome of a preteen sleepover—girls rolled up in fuzzy pajama pants, happily eating kettle corn, and separating movie discs into small piles while the latest pop noise droned through iPod speakers. I never really fit into these things because I was too much of a "tomboy" to fully enjoy all the gossip and hair braiding. But I was there nonetheless.

Over time, I had mostly gotten used to my constant separation, but I never fully adapted to the most alienating of situations. There were always those few, endless moments when I wanted to completely disappear. These were the famous lines out of every teen girl book or movie—the times when I was truly scared, and would be even more silent than usual. When my friends discussed their crushes, all on averagely cute, young boys, I tried my hardest to sink into the nearest wall. It was my cue to remove myself from the conversation, simply to smile and nod like I related to the topic. I knew I could never bring up a girl's name to disrupt the flowing string of, "Johnny so looked at me today!"

A confession of my true feelings would thoroughly set me apart and break the thin ties connecting me to my friends. I didn't want to destroy the shiny lacquer of female expectations that we had all been coated in since birth. This was already cracked from how I felt about the other "normal girl" things. I hated the Jonas Brothers, despised the Disney princesses, and had constant impulses to throw mud at anything glittery. An absolute abomination.

I cringed at the almost endless supply of trendy teen magazines lying all over the floor and clutched in my friends' pink-polished fingers. Hot men with airbrushed, teenage faces covered every page of the booklets. Groomed, glossy, chiseled jaws and perfect hair to match. They were clones, with eyes that could easily drill into the mind of a trembling girl.

My middle school peers giggled and pointed at all the pictures, just like girls are supposed to. But I just sat aside frigidly, biting my nails, and trying to avert my eyes from the flat, deliberate gaze of the men. They stared into me darkly, as if they knew what was wrong with me, and eventually started to tell me so.

"Ooh you wanna be with me, huh? Come here girl, let me turn you. Look at me, not my hot model trophy wife."

Simple things like this nibbled at my mind and made me want to rip my hair out.

As a questioning twelve-year-old, my open mindset was a-okay with my possible homosexuality. But when I really looked at the world around me, and how different I was from everyone else, I pushed myself far back behind the murky closet door. Besides, who would believe me anyway? Some people just didn't get the existence of early bloomers in this whole sexuality thing. Hell—when I was eight years old, I kissed almost every member of my Girl Scout troop. Not once did I ever consider it being out of the ordinary.

So when my older sister told me I looked like an "ugly dyke" based on my rugged outfits, I did not know what to think. I knew ugly was something very bad, but the other word was where my world started to get muddled. This word "dyke" refers to women who love other women (with a negative connotation, I might add). And as I came to realize this, I was terrified. If my own sister wasn't a fan of gay people, how would everyone else come to terms with it? How could I even deal with it? This was the first time I contemplated the fact that my curiosity had the possibility of turning out very badly.

As I got older, and started to know for sure that I did not like boys, these problems grew. I heard the slurs thrown around in the school halls, and I tried so hard not to listen. But they seemed to chase after me wherever I went. The hateful notes left in my locker were tiny grenades that exploded over and over, the bombshell debris leaving a constant, melancholy weight in my chest. That was all I was to my peers. Not a person, and not even an object. Just some useless words on a page.

I started to torture myself, and used the Internet as a tool to degrade my own identity. I saw all the articles on hate crimes and suicide. I dug up every picture of a slur-splattered poster being held in an oblivious child's hands. I discovered that nine out of ten LGBTQ+ teens are bullied in school, and that we're three times more likely to throw ourselves off a cliff or hang ropes around our necks. I realized that the words tossed back and forth in my middle school compared better to loaded guns than letters of the alphabet. I realized that there were so many sad, scared gay kids, and too many already six feet under. I didn't want to be there with them.

I not only wanted to be proud and happy, but also to help others get there, too. I craved a feeling of being content with myself, and was suddenly determined to get to that state. I searched for positive LGBTQ+ communities on the Internet, and found so much support on many websites. My favorite source was the diverse groups on Tumblr, a powerhouse safe haven of accepting and flamboyant people of all sexualities and genders. I even discovered that some of my real-life friends were queer as well, which put me on cloud nine. It turned out I was never alone in the first place.

So, of course, I decided to come out. I didn't yell it off rooftops or throw a rainbow parade. It was more of a gradual process. I answered people when they asked, and told my family of my minor difference, to which they did not object.

Most importantly I accepted myself, and that no matter what, I couldn't change.

Today, I am an optimistic blast of rainbow, ready to take on the world. I proudly support and help everyone in the LGBTQ+ community in and outside of school. I am one of the strong leaders of the Gay-Straight Alliance, and work to promote tolerance and love everywhere I go. I never thought I could do any of this. My minority status used to bring me down, but now it's like a superpower. What I once thought was the end, is truly only the beginning.

We have all been afraid of who we are, and we have all felt alone. Of course, even though I'll have to face a few more homophobes and be alienated for who I love from time to time, the battle with myself is over. I am extremely lucky to be here and lucky to love who I am. And when I look back at all my self-hatred and those moments at the sleepovers, I will be proud. Proud to represent all the kids who didn't make it through, and to lend a helping hand to those still struggling.

My Life, My Nature

MARIANGEL NATI DELGADO * *age 12*
Saint James School

Water is my life and my way of identifying myself and I'd love to control it with my hands. I won't use it for self-defense, I'd rather use it for fun in the summer. Water can also be romantic: imagine yourself on an island surrounded by water on your honeymoon. Now that's romantic.

This may be a reason why we don't need water to be controlled: it's also nature, nature is not supposed to be controlled. It should stay for everyone to enjoy because nature (water) is unique, one, calm, breathtaking, and beautiful. Remember — NATURE IS NOT CONTROLLED. Not earth, not air, and not fire.

Let things be.

Camping

EVELYN FLORES ✴ *age 8*
Sanchez Elementary School

Two weeks ago, I went camping with my dad, mom, two sisters, two cousins, and two dogs. One dog was really flawless, and it was white and little. The dog was nice and really liked me. He kept following me the whole time. When I got there, I ate breakfast and went to the water, and the water was warm. I know how to swim.

I got on the Jet Ski with my uncle, and he was training to make ginormous waves. There was a crash in the water because my uncle was trying so hard to make waves. The Jet Ski went on top of a boat, but there was only a little scratch. But my uncle put red tape on the boat, because he did not want to see the scratch. Nobody was hurt. We stayed for two weeks. The water tasted like fish and dirt. The waves were like crocodiles.

Surviving with Half a Brain

JULES JAMISON * *age 16*
John O'Connell High School

The human brain is split into two halves. Each half is responsible for its own list of functions. The right side controls the left side of your body, and the left side of the brain controls the right side of your body. The human brain is also academically split. Things like reading and language fall to the left side of the brain. Subjects like math and music respond to the right side of the brain.

The human body is like a well-oiled machine, but what happens when the communication center isn't working right and you are brain damaged? Well, other things stop working correctly. Every motion you make, even simple tasks like moving a finger or blinking an eye, have to start at the brain before they can happen. This means that if your brain is damaged, your whole body is damaged.

My story starts from the day I was born into this world. I was born under unfortunate conditions: the umbilical cord was wrapped tightly around my neck, making it impossible to breathe. This was only the beginning of a chain reaction of drastic changes in my life that have made me the person I am today.

The first three years of my life were fantastic. I loved to run around outside and sit—more like stand—in the driver's seat of any car and pretend to drive. Then an unexpected thing happened when I was about three and a half: I tripped and fell to the ground. I got back up with no injuries, but I did have a newly-acquired limp in my right leg. I didn't show any signs that I had hurt myself, so my mother assumed that my limp would just go away eventually. Unfortunately, the limp didn't subside. In fact, I started to have odd mood changes. I became scared of heights. I stopped going outside, and all I wanted to do was sit in the dark, safe, TV room. Eventually, my parents began taking me to many specialists to figure out what had happened to me. When I finally got an MRI, or a picture of the brain, I was diagnosed with hydrocephalus. I had brain surgery two days later.

The condition I have is called *hydrocephalus*. In other words, I had water on my brain. (*Hydro*, meaning water, and *cephalus*, meaning brain). In order to drain the excess brain fluid, the doctors put a shunt, or water pump, into my head. They also stuck a tube up through my stomach and going up through my throat, which connected to the shunt. The fluid would be pumped down through the tube and into my urinary system. If it weren't for that surgery, I probably wouldn't be here today.

Just two days after the surgery, I was back to laughing and jumping on my bed with utter joy. My mother said, "It's like the life just came back." I began to go outside and heights were no problem. The only thing that didn't change was the oddly acquired limp. To this day, I have to compensate for my weakness on my right side.

I was five years old when I started kindergarten in the small town of Graton. I wasn't much different than most of the kids in my class, but as I went through the elementary grades, the effects of my brain injury became quite clear.

I have vivid memories of sitting in class with the textbook in front of me. Every time a reader stopped and the teacher started to pick another reader, my teeth clenched. It felt like the harder I hoped not to be picked, the more often it happened. Every time I stumbled on a word, about five other students corrected me in the meanest way, like I was dumb. I tried to tell the teacher that I could not read out loud in front of the class, but he or she would just say things like, "Everyone has their weaknesses" or "Practice makes perfect." I went completely insane. It made me feel completely unheard and annoyed by the people who were supposed to understand.

Another struggle I faced, and am still facing, was physical. The pressure on my brain had caused damage to the nerves controlling my right side. Walking was three times harder for me, and when it came to balance, I had none. I constantly tripped over my right foot, and would always hear "hee hee" from my classmates. Sometimes it was silent, but most of the time it was the blatant laughter of judgment. People asked me to race because I would never win. After beating me, they ran around like they had a stick up their leg and yelled, "I'm Jules, everyone. Look!"

Although in this life I have been given many challenges, the outcomes have not been all bad. I excel at music, and now play three instruments. Math has always been a comfort zone for me. So even though I was slow at many things and people made fun of my lack of ability, it made my strengths that much stronger.

As a student with brain damage, I have had to overcome lots of hurdles. I wish that it was easier to explain the effects of brain and nerve damage to people without these characteristics, but words can't explain as well as experiences. It took me twice as long to reach the "norm," or what people expected of me. A lot of the people around me didn't make it any easier, and I became discouraged a lot of the time. Even in those moments, I believed that my brain didn't hinder me, but instead gave me a reason to try harder. So to those who know what it's like to be in my shoes, don't let this stop you from your dreams. Help others understand our situation. For everyone else, remember there is always a reason for everything, and assuming can only get you so far.

Life of a Soldier

JETNIPA CHAROENPORNPOJ ✷ *age 16*
John O'Connell High School

Being a soldier is hard, and of course, no one wants to be
a soldier. You don't want to fight; you don't want to die; and
you don't want to endure the pain. In Thailand (and probably
other countries as well), when you reach the age of fifteen
you have to report to the Army Reserve Force training for
three years. It is mostly to avoid being drafted into the full-
fledged military.

Everything begins with tiny little steps. When you are in
grade one, you are forced to join the Boy Scouts. Of course,
that doesn't sound like it has anything to do with the army, but
the formations they use are the same as the ones in soldier
training! Fast-forward a few years to middle school, where
they make you go to the jungle to learn about nature and
survival—what can and can't be eaten, how to start a camp-
fire, how to hunt, etc. All of these skills are used when you are
a soldier. The Boy Scout year ends when you reach the age of
fourteen, but this is really just the beginning.

I'm in the first year of training (private first class), and it
is already hard. Before you join the training, you have to take
a physical education test to see if you can pass. It includes
running half a mile within three minutes, twenty-two push-
ups, and thirty-three sit-ups in under three minutes. Almost
one-third of people fail and must wait until the following year

to try again. If you can't pass all of the trainings by the time you reach the age of twenty-two, you are forced to join the army. This means staying at the soldier barracks all the time and training there for three years. I almost failed.

My first day at training wasn't so bad. The drill sergeant just tells you what you are expected to do for one year. On the second day, we begin formation training, which lasts for a few months, and then comes physical training. You have to run, even in the hot sun or pouring rain. They either give you a rifle or an assault rifle filled with enough bullets to kill someone. You have to crawl past barbed wire, do the zip line, and wear a suit and helmet that is incredibly heavy. The smell of gunpowder, and the sound of guns were everywhere, but overall it is a fun time. Being a soldier is not that bad until you get sent to war, or to the frontier.

From what I've heard from people, near the end of every year of training, they send you to the rainforest up on the mountain for one week of training on how to survive, how to hunt, and also some combat tactics. Everyone was scared of wild animals and scared of the jungle because they had never been there. The sound of wild animals and insects around the camp are enough to scare full-grown men.

Every male in Thailand is born to be a soldier. Of course we have other jobs too, and you aren't forced to do anything after training. You can go back to your normal life. But in times of war, we are called to fight as the second line of defense. We just hope it never happens. But if it ever happens, we are ready for it. The training might be hard, and it might give us a rough time, but it makes us stronger. We come to understand how important the training is. We never want to go to training thinking it will be useless. You never know when you are going to need it.

The Great Soccer Game

DIEGO GAMBALA ✳ *age 8*
Buena Vista Horace Mann

After a whole year, we were going to the *Copa del Oro*. We were all excited. Our coach was also excited. Jose is my coach. All the boys are eight or nine. My dad and I drove to the smelly, fake turf. The game started. I was excited. I saw kids in black jerseys everywhere. Immediately, they made two goals. We all felt nervous. We switched our goalie out and worked harder. I started to get sweaty. I passed the ball to Joshua, and he made a goal. The referee blew the whistle. It was half time.

I ran to my dad to get some water and a snack. The ref blew the whistle again. I ran to my position and got into my stance. We started with the ball. Diego passed the ball to me. I scored a goal. Then Joshua stole the ball and made a goal. "There are only five minutes to go," said Coach. We were going to win. The game finished. We won! Later, we had the party of a lifetime. It was as awesome as a red komodo dragon.

The Arrow that Broke My Heart

HAN WANG * *age 17*
Albany High School

Swoosh! Out went the arrow, a falcon seeking its prey. Through the cracks of the protection I once thought invincible, the arrow directly hit my pride, my happiness, my life. It destroyed the very part of my spirit that kept a smile on my face. I couldn't believe it. I couldn't make myself believe that she'd said it, the last words that escaped her beautiful lips: "I HATE YOU, HATE YOU!"

Just because I had driven another girl home. She thought it wasn't that simple. She said that she would never trust me ever again. I knew our love was changing. The truth had been edging into my consciousness for a long time. The tone of her voice as she spoke to me and the diminishing amount of time we spent together felt like a dark cloud miles away, but slowly closing in on me. All of a sudden, the cloud drenched my weary body.

Like lightning, in a flash, I recalled the happy moments we'd spent together: meeting each other, our first date, our first kiss. Then came the thunder, rumbling, signaling the doom of our relationship. The sound of happiness collapsing. I was lost, exhausted. I stumbled back home and threw myself onto the bed, struggling to fall asleep, to leave the merciless world on this stormy day. As I closed my eyes, her face haunted my brain.

Her lips, as pure as fresh air in a forest never before seen by humans, were now polluted by words full of hate. I opened my eyes to free my mind of this torture, but her face was on the ceiling, in the mirror, on the floor. I squeezed my pillow, rolling around the bed, trying to shake her out of my thoughts, without success. My cellphone rang. It was her. A light penetrated the clouds in my heart. Maybe all was okay. I picked up the phone with hope and tried to explain again how she dominated my heart. She wouldn't believe me and hung up the phone, which I dropped in despair, knowing we were through.

After two days without her, I felt free, like a parakeet out of her cage. Two days of reflecting on my own had taught me that I wasn't mature enough to fall into the cage of love. She called again. I didn't care, I left it ringing. The insincerity in her first call had done irreparable damage and left a scar that would never disappear. She wouldn't be the same and I would not heal. Hardened, I emerged out of the storm.

After all, life is a peaceful river. It wouldn't be special without a few jagged rocks, creating magnificent splashes. Afterwards, all is calm. Silence falls upon the river, peacefully traveling down, waiting for the next rock to show its beauty.

Happy Shadows

MILTON STOOKEY * *age 14*
International High School

I lost my best friend to a stroke of bad luck. Well, I didn't exactly lose him. Florian and I are still in touch, I guess. Seven years after he left, we do still exchange emails every now and then. It just would be so much better if he were here. Now we're both fourteen and have spent most of our lives apart—do we even have anything in common anymore? I sigh, and sink back into memory. Suddenly, I'm small; nothing's lost yet—

It was a warm evening in October 2007. I was over at Florian's. We were having a sleepover. Excited, we buzzed about the house, playing with his toys, having a great time like only kids can. The air licked us, bathing us in humid warmth. We decided it would be fun to go out. We grabbed a soccer and a tennis ball from his closet, and headed for the door. Chattering across the front yard, our shadows mingled with the evening environment, but although darkness was coming on, there was no fear here. Together, we were encapsulated in a bubble of friendship, young and safe from all troubles.

Florian lived in a quiet, residential neighborhood of Oakland. Small cottages lined the thin gray of cracked pavement as far as the eye could see, and trees sprouted here and there, casting green shadows over the mute townscape. Across from his house there was a large school complex. At the center the buildings huddled together, like the bull's-eye of a target, and around them was a big, open-air playing area. There was a clumpy, browning field, and a chiseled basketball court—lined cement upholding netless hoops, a worthy landmark to this age-worn place.

We skipped eagerly toward the complex. The sky had lost its watercolor blue to something deeper, but near the horizon there remained a distinct lightness that enabled us to see; perhaps behind the distant skyscrapers of San Francisco, to the west, a sliver of fire still lived. An orange rectangle flicked on behind us as we approached the street.

"Florian, sweetie, remember to look both ways, and run across quickly!" his mother, Agna, chirped from the kitchen window.

Asserting our maturity, we shrugged, and peeking to the left and to the right, dashed across the quiet strip. She watched us, silhouetted in a rectangle of warmth and safety.

Safely on the other side, we eyed our next obstacle. The school's perimeter was surrounded by a large chain-link fence.

"Lets climb it," Florian said as I hesitated. "Look, it's easy, I do it all the time."

He launched the balls over, and they bounced softly to a halt on the other side. Then, he began to ascend, and it seemed easy enough, so I grabbed hold of the fence and began to drag myself up too. The cold steel bored painfully into my fingers, but I was determined to succeed. Finally, we reached the top.

"Now what?" I asked.

Florian motioned to watch him. He carefully maneuvered over the spiky links till he had both heels securely nestled into chinks on the other side. "Weeeeeeeee!" He screamed, and let go with a kick. He dropped five feet and crumbled laughing onto the grass.

"See Milton? It's easy! Just go slowly, and then jump! It's like flying."

I was nervous, but I managed to work all ten toes over the top and into safe positions. "Just jump?" I stammered, nervous. It was high up there.

"Yeah. Trust me, you'll be fine." I looked at the sky for support.

"Okay," I let go, spinning, and the deep blue was no more. I felt the swish of fast air around me and the cool sudden softness of fibrous grass. "Owwww," I exhaled, giggling. I turned over, and was looking into Florian's brown face. We smiled at each other. He stood up, brushing off dirt, so I did too.

"Come on, let's go! What do you want to do first?"

"Let's play soccer."

In agreement, we crossed to opposite sides of the field. I used the evenly spaced fence posts as my goal, and we pooled our striped sweaters to create his. I punted the soccer ball into the air at random, to begin the game. Adrenaline filled me, and I was immediately streaking toward the spinning ball. We were two blurs in a desperate chase. I reached it first, and looked up with just enough time to see Florian sprinting at me, hands flat like slabs of pita to improve aerodynamics (this was a secret of ours, and we were both very fast. Coincidence? You tell me!) With the agility of an ice skater, I cut the ball to the side and dodged the wildly blowing hair of the human cannonball. My own hair, heavy, straight, blond to his wild, curly, black, flapped chaotically with a life of its own, and life became a race with the speeding ground.

He had doubled back, and gained on me as he had no ball to dribble. Neck and neck. Unconsciously, I turned my head to look as I ran, and my flushed face saw his. We shot forward together. The ball swerved between our feet, a colorless shape in the darkening surroundings. His goal was becoming nearer. He was ahead of me now, turning around. I slowed down. He came at me again, confident in his actions. I tried to turn, but felt the ball resist. I looked down—he had taken it away. He turned with the ball, and I was scared. I was tiring. Desperate, I reached as far as I could, and with the tip of my outstretched toe, managed to poke it away from him again. I was once again in possession of the ball, but he was coming at me. It was now or never. At the last second, I kicked it with all my might. We both squinted into the darkness. Behind Florian, a speeding shadow raced across the torn earth, and came to rest on the other side of his goal.

"Gooooooaal!" I shouted uncontrollably.

We paused a few seconds to regain our breath, then began again. Ten more minutes we played, then got bored. I had had a glorious victory of sixteen to nine. Then, with the sun's last fingers creeping back from the horizon, we jogged over to the basketball courts and tossed the soccer ball at the frayed net, like a monster bug at a very worn spider web. It was still light enough to see, so we packed in the baskets, then got bored again and broke out the tennis ball, throwing it to each other as far as we could. Sprint and catch the piece of fuzzy green at full throttle, feel the wind and the heavy air, the coolness of space and the night. Eventually, it became too dark even to toss or kick it to each other, so we abandoned it. But everything was so nice, and we still had energy to use.

We had the idea at the same time.

"RACE YOU BACK!" We were off like crazed atoms, running less for the pleasure of competition than for the wind, the smells of the night, the flying sensation of freedom. We swerved back and forth, crisscrossing each other, reaching the fence but unsatisfied, turning around again and shooting back into the dusk, around and around and around—heaving chests, we finally collapsed into breathless happiness, indefinable, yet so pure. Then we just lay there and laughed for a beautiful eternity. Finally, in near absolute darkness, pierced only by the raw streetlamps, we rose shivering and weak.

"That was so fun! Ahhhhhh." I heaved a sigh of satisfaction.

"It must be getting late. Let's go back home."

Side by side, we stumbled back through the night to the fence that barred our exit, a monstrous knight in chain mail. But we knew it wouldn't hurt us. We clambered over it together, two seasoned climbers, and carefully looked in both directions before fording the street. The orange rectangle remained lit. There was no face in it now watching us. We toiled up the garden path to the door, which was unlocked.

"There you are! You were out there for ages! Come in quickly and eat something! It's 7:30, almost your bedtime!"

We were assaulted by the pungent smells of home cooking. Agna guided us into the small kitchen dining area, where Florian's dad, Julian, was sitting and reading a thick book. He glanced up momentarily, and then went back to his read. We seated ourselves on rickety chairs in the warm orange light, sharply contrasting to the darkness outside. The light made me feel safe, but outside in the dark with my friend, I knew we had felt safe anyway. The cool, crusty macaroni slipped down my hungry throat, although I didn't like it, and my full belly began to make me sleepy. Agna gave us a soy vanilla ice cream sandwich, a chez-Florian special which I loved, and two gummy vitamins apiece to help it down. After we'd finished, she herded us into the bathroom. She yelled at Florian to brush his teeth, hunted around for a toothbrush for me, watched as I spread it with Monster's Inc. flavored toothpaste and slipped it into my mouth, pretending to like the flavor. I'd always preferred mint.

Finally, our evening drawing to a close, we crawled, beaten, into Florian's small, closet-sized room. The dark space was littered with Pokémon cards and toys, and a cramped loft bed took up the right wall. We both clambered up into it, lying down with our feet facing each other. Agna and Julian came in turn, kissed Florian, said goodnight to me; then, as Julian left, he flicked the switch beside Florian's door. The orange abruptly disappeared, the door closed, and I found myself in complete darkness. Even breathing filled the room, and despite the darkness, which alone would have been menacing, I felt safe.

Six months later, Florian moved away to China. His mom, who worked for Leapfrog, had been transferred. I couldn't understand why he had to go. I wanted him to stay here. She could move to China if she wanted. It never really occurred to me that he was leaving until he was gone. The last time I saw him, at the end-of-year school celebration, he seemed fine, normal. We ran about as usual, and although I felt an undercurrent of urgency, I didn't show it and neither did he. I only partially realized that I wouldn't see him again in years. When it finally came time to say goodbye, we hugged and clung to each other like magnets. Come on, Milton, I thought. I have it easy. He's moving to China. But it was still too much. That last hug, and brave teary smile, then his striped sweater being jerked away through the crowd—only then I understood I had lost who I most cared about.

I searched the schoolyard frantically with my eyes, found nothing, and suddenly, sprinted toward the exit. I had to find him! I had to! But I couldn't. A knight in chain-mail, who suddenly seemed very tall, barred my exit. And without Florian, I couldn't climb... I was trapped. Suddenly, from around the block a flash caught my eye. He was running back. I was delirious. An adult opened the gate for us and we hugged one last, beautiful time. Then his parents pulled up beside the curb, motioned him in. In my arms, he looked up at me and tried to convey that we would always remain friends. But his eyes were tearing up now. He was embarrassed, and looked away. Finally, we broke apart; he turned and sprinted into the vehicle. The doors closed, Julian and Agna waved, and the car turned the corner and was gone. He was gone. A long moment passed in silence. Suddenly, I was running again. Running fast, back through the crowd, to a corner under the play structure that seemed secret. There my tears sprang from my eyes, and grew exponentially from droplets to a stream to buckets and buckets of warm, salty sadness. The grief pounded on my mind like a hammer, a physical pain, and I cradled myself— waiting, powerless, as an ocean I didn't know existed poured out of me. All thoughts were wiped away, until finally, nothing remained of me but a shivering husk. The celebration was over. I sat in a puddle of my own tears. My parents came and I hardened my shell, bracing myself. We drove home. In another car, fifteen miles away and reaching the airport, he was crying too. But I knew nothing of that.

Attention: those who are reading this book on a tight schedule that does not allow time for rising action, climax, and denouement (those take forever), or those who have tricked their friends into a who-can-read-a-section-of-the-826-Quarterly-the-fastest competition (those are fun). Here's a hint: read this section. It features the several projects we did this fall with middle-school students, in which they wrote long pieces and then polished perfect little excerpts to a high shine, as well as a few stand-out, stand-alone, stand-up-straight-or-you'll-get-stuck-that-way snippets of longer writing. Ready, get set…go.

Jumbly, Gloriumptious

Excerpts

Roller Coaster

STEPHANIE CASTRO * *age 13*
James Lick Middle School

I started screaming and my stomach felt like butterflies; it's the same feeling I get when I get on a swing and
close my eyes.

Pig Soccer

MILES BUHRMANN ✳ *age 13*
James Lick Middle School

A group of three pigs huddled together and slowly approached the ball. Then, one brave pig stepped forward and nudged it with its snout. And just like that, all the pigs crowded forward.

Exploding Boots

OLIVIA BAKER * *age 13*
Beacon Day School

It was the day my boots exploded. They weren't on me of course, that would have been dangerous. Though now that I think about it, the whole point of the explosion was to cause danger, therefore causing excitement. I lived in a boring old town whose name I don't care enough about to remember. I hated the town with every last single particle in me. I mean, what's a girl to do when the town's idea of fun is homework, and the nearest thing to a rebel was that boy in sixth grade who didn't tuck in his shirt? I would have done anything for excitement, so I did what any person would have done. I set my boots on fire. Who was I to know that they would explode, causing Mr. Brown to drop his keys down the gutter in surprise, and causing Mrs. O'Brien's wig to catch on fire? It's not my fault, if you really think about it. Who stands next to a bored teenage girl with a match?

Screaming Inside

CARLOS NOGUERA * *age 13*
Everett Middle School

So I walked straight to the back of the bus. There were at least three people in the back: one Latino, one African American, and one old white guy. The guy was staring at me for at least five minutes. Finally he spoke, "How would you like to be my personal gardener?!" he asked.

I said no. With anger I said, "Why would you say that? Because of my skin color?"

He said, "You're brown and Mexican."

I said, "No, I'm Nicaraguan."

Then he said, "Do you want to make eight dollars an hour?"

I felt ashamed of my culture for a while. The old guy was still talking, saying, "Come on, I bet your family would do this." I felt like punching this guy in the face. I was screaming inside my body, but I know not to punch somebody in the face.

Jumbly, Gloriumptious

TAIG LONERGAN * *age 13*
Everett Middle School

In that moment, I felt more free than a prisoner getting let out of jail. Though it was a jumbly, gloriumptious pleasure, we decided that if we had to take showers every time we wrestled in the mud, we wouldn't want to play outside anymore. Yet, we were grateful that we had not just stayed inside. We were joyous as we ignored the rest of the world.

"Let's play sports tomorrow," I suggested. Everyone nodded vigorously at my idea.

Now, I realize that I should value these rare, monumental moments. Though it only felt like an exciting day, I've learned that there is so much more significance to these memories than it seems.

Untitled

NELL DAYTON-JOHNSON ✳ *age 16*
Cypress High School

My social worker had placed me with the last standing members of my family, who happened to live in the same apartment. My new government-given Brady Bunch included my paternal grandparents, my great uncle, and my dad's baby sister, my aunt. The apartment was situated on a busy street in Midtown, in a neighborhood that was neither safe nor dangerous. The building was a bright green that made me uncomfortable. It stood out amongst the monochromatic buildings like that nauseating flappy mole on grandma's neck. The inside of the apartment smelled like the result of fifteen years of chain smoking and baking casserole in a Bed, Bath and Beyond. The rooms were over-decorated, featuring clashing patterns, shag rugs, and my grandmother's nude painting of Bill Clinton. Yellowing doilies hung in the windows, serving as a net for Grandpa's cigarette ash and great-uncle Irving's stray psoriasis.

It Smelled Like Gum

MIGUEL ANGEL VILLALOBOS ✳ *age 13*
Everett Middle School

On my first day in my new school, City Academic, on the white walls were pictures of all the students. There were just white people and it smelled like gum in the white walls. The sun was too bright and hot, and when I entered in the school, it was cold and smelled like all things were raw. There was a new bright, big photo of a team of basketball players that won the championship last year. The team was tall and all white, like polar bears in ice.

The Danger of Asking Valid Questions

NATE HOPE * *age 13*
James Lick Middle School

After my mom was called, I wasn't allowed to play video-games until I finished the book *Watership Down*, which I found to be unfathomably boring. I think I'd rather have my eyes gouged out with ice cream scoops.

Damp Fog

ORLA AYTON * *age 13*
Everett Middle School

It all began halfway through summer break. As usual, all of the kids raced outside to recess. We hurried through the first floor corridor, and out of the double doors. The sky was dark and gray, and I could feel the damp fog on my face. It doesn't matter to me; this is the perfect weather.

The Heat of Hunger

ASHANTE WILLIAMS * *age 18*
Downtown High School

Scrounger is the smartest female black bear I know, and out of all the lady bears I have come across, she is the finest. Even though many black bears are brown instead of black, her light brown eyes, which compliment her sandy brown fur, are what caught my attention. Her extreme memory of where to find hidden food sources is what keeps me around.

Fred the Skateboarder

DIEGO CRISTERNA * *age 8*
Buena Vista Horace Mann

Fred also had a dog named Skate who had supersonic hearing and could smell for one kilometer. Skate had razor-sharp teeth to help protect Fred. Skate wore a tuxedo. Fred was a hipster. Fred was doing a cool trick in Texas and he was almost bitten by a double-tailed rattlesnake. But his dog, Skate, saved the day and ate the snake.

The Runaway

RASHAAD SIMPSON-WHITE ✳ *age 13*
James Lick Middle School

My feet pounded, boom! boom! like a stampede of rhinos.
I hit the door, and the hot breezy air hit my face like I was in
heaven. I was finally free, like a bird.

Too Many Stairs to the Library

HAZEL DRAKE * *age 13*
James Lick Middle School

Librarians usually seem to be friendly. I picked up a book and read it as fast as I eat ice cream. In a way, I took pieces of other characters and made them part of myself. I am a book that hasn't been written.

Journey to the Water

BRAYAM MAGANA * *age 17*
Downtown High School

Her feet are made to live by the water, webbed feet that are meant to swim, but today they will be used as an instrument to climb, if she can find a way. She hears a bush shaking and little branches breaking behind her. Scared, she jumps and turns around, but it is a squirrel and he pays no attention to her. She isn't his target; he wants a berry. She doesn't look at him as a threat either. He turns, fills his mouth and runs up the tree. She studies him. He is using his claws to climb the tree. She follows him, jumping from one tree to another. The squirrel stops and Brown examines the area. Seeing a small waterfall flowing into a stream, she jumps. Her instinct is to follow the stream.

My First Crush

SAVANNAH BATTLE * *age 13*
James Lick Middle School

The boy I was crushing on had soft, silky black hair, brown, blazing eyes that brought a smile to my face and warmth to my heart, teeth that shone bright like a diamond, and the body of a god! He smelled as if a cloud of Axe was following him. He was every girl's Monday and Friday.

A Writer's Mirror

NICOLE FLORES ✳ *age 12*
James Lick Middle School

I would walk slowly in the sand and narrate a catchy, juicy line in my head: "I walked slowly in the hot sand, which was now beginning to cool down because of the gentle breeze that also blew on my long, curly brown hair. Against the golden sunshine it looked like shiny copper chains." This is the story of how my mind flew across the mirrors of my heart.

And also some other questions: what's up with education in California? Where did this crazy drought come from and what are we supposed to do about it? How does one become a professional comic artist before one is old enough to get a driver's license? How is immigration reform affecting kids? Who's better, the Giants or the Dodgers? What do people ages eight to fifteen find newsworthy? What are they going to write about next? Should we ever stop asking questions?

Now I Pose One Final Question

Journalism

Death by Drought

BEN FRIEDMAN-HIBBS * *age 11*
Rooftop School

Sure, we've all heard about the drought. It is causing a dry spell with very little rain, and it is drying out the landscape. But there is one terrifying fact that most people don't know: the drought is literally MOVING us! According to NASA, "So much groundwater has disappeared — much of it from pumping to farms — that it's causing the state to shrink in mass."

Now, you may be thinking, *Why should I care if there is a drought?* There are a few simple answers. First, the obvious one: humans, animals, and plants all need water. Then there are some that we take for granted. We could lose precious things we use daily, such as taking showers and washing dishes. The final point: we could lose our crops and not have enough food.

According to smithsonian.com, "The record-breaking California drought is so bad that monitoring stations used to study earthquakes can detect the drying ground rising up. Measurements of these subtle movements, made using GPS instruments, suggest that the western United States is missing some 62 trillion gallons of water, enough to cover the entire region six inches deep." So there you have it: we are rising AND shrinking.

Another thought that may be going through your mind is, *How can I tell the difference between hot weather and a drought?* According to Juliet Christian-Smith, a climate scientist with the Union of Concerned Scientists, "The difference between hot/dry weather and a drought is that 'drought' means a dry period bad enough to have social, environmental, or economic effects. In other words, droughts occur when people or the environment suffers from water shortages."

Are there different classifications of droughts? Christian-Smith says, "Yes, the U.S. Drought Monitor has four different drought classifications. Most of California is currently in an exceptional drought, which means that there are 'exceptional and widespread crop/pasture losses and shortages of water in reservoirs, streams, and wells creating water emergencies.' California is in the highest level of drought, called a D4.

How do droughts affect us? Christian-Smith says, "Droughts often mean that people who live in cities and towns have to conserve water by not watering lawns or washing cars, taking shorter showers, and turning off the tap while we brush our teeth. Droughts also mean that farmers have less water to grow food."

What does it mean that the drought is shrinking California? Christian-Smith says, "If you think about the ground as a sponge, when we have a lot of water it sinks into the ground and fills up the sponge. When we pump water out of the ground and we don't have a lot of rain, the sponge can dry up. When the 'sponge' of the soil dries up it shrinks a little; we can detect this shrinkage when we see that the land is dropping in certain places where it is very dry and we are pumping a lot of water out of the ground."

Now I pose one final question: How can we stop this drought? Christian-Smith says "Use water wisely; when we use less water, there is more water to go around. Most of the water that we use in California is used outdoors, to grow crops and to water lawns; therefore it is particularly important to find ways to minimize outdoor water use. For instance, some people have 'drought-tolerant lawns' that have plants that use less water instead of grass."

So now that you've heard this, will you take a long shower tonight? Will YOU use the extra water?

Kids Caught Up in Immigration Mess

DANIEL MARTINEZ * *age 13*
Everett Middle School

Children should be loved, not traumatized. This is especially true at our southern border, where kids are being
threatened by gangs and drug dealers. They are moved to live
in spaces that are too small to house all of them. There is little
space for the kids to sleep, and the camp looks unsanitary.
Instead of being kept at the border, they should be allowed to
cross into the U.S.

Federal agents are holding the immigrant children for
seventy-two hours before transferring them to Housing and
Human Services (HHS). Are these the right people to do
the job? Not likely, as border patrol's job is not to deal with
the children. These agents believe it is a better job for child
welfare experts, because they are trained to do this.

Yet, according to Wendy Young of Kids in Need of Defense
(KIND), an advocacy group for unaccompanied immigrant
kids, "The current system Congress put in place was designed
for about 6,000 to 8,000 kids a year, not the numbers we're
seeing now." Despite everything bad at the border, many
families believe their children will have a better life in the
U.S. According to Ana Herrera, a San Francisco immigration attorney, "What would improve the situation is a better

immigration bill. If Congress doesn't pass one, the president probably will."

Something needs to be done soon. These kids deserve a better life than the one they left.

Bullying: Who's to Blame?

ROSA CRUZ * *age 14*
Mission High School

"This is a systematic problem and we're all contributing to it," wrote Randy Taran, founder of Project Happiness. I am talking about bullying and who's to blame. People say that only the bully is to blame, but I think everyone has a part.

I think everyone contributes to bullying in some way. When people don't speak up or stand up for each other, they're making the problem bigger. It's important for the victim to speak up, but it's hard for them because they are sometimes afraid or don't have support from friends or adults. When a teacher or a counselor just focuses on the victim, that's not making much of a change; the bully will go on to bully other people. I feel like the victim and the bully should get equal attention.

According to an article about bullying by Eric Weddle, in 2013, 44 percent of bullying incidents were verbal incidents and 21 percent were physical incidents. There were 9,396 incidents reported, but some schools are so afraid of "looking bad" that they don't report bullying. Middle schools were reported to have most incidents. Schools are also a part of the problem because they usually just suspend the bully and tell the victim that everything will be okay. But will it really? The bully will usually keep bullying other people or not care.

At Mission High School, they have a Wellness Center in which they give support to the victim and counseling to the bully. I interviewed Chandra Sivakumar from the Mission High Wellness Center and he said, "Let your voice be heard." If you're involved in a bullying situation, someone from the Wellness Center will sit down with you to determine what's going on, how you're feeling, and to figure out what's causing the problem. They will look into the emotional side, because the consequences of bullying can be depression or suicide. It affects students because they are so focused on rumors and being talked about that they don't focus on school. They fail a class, they face academic problems and stress—it's a cycle: from bullying to stress to failing school to more stress, and then that causes even more bullying which leads to thoughts that sadly sometimes lead to death.

Bullies usually bully because of insecurities, or because they themselves are victims of bullying. I asked Chandra, "Do you think we all contribute to bullying?", and he responded by saying, "I'm not sure we all contribute to bullying." I disagree with him. I feel like when bystanders watch and don't do anything, they're contributing by not helping the person. When I say "person," I mean both the bully and the victim. When bullies gets caught, schools will usually get them suspended or give them expulsion if it's really bad. I feel like that doesn't help at all. They're not doing anything to stop the problem. At the Wellness Center, they will support you and try to see what's going on outside of school or at home.

The best way to solve this problem would be for everyone to be able to speak up and report when bullying is happening, and for both the bully and the victim to get equal attention from friends and adults. In his article, Weddle writes that teachers are now getting trained on how to see signs of bullying happening. They also have to report it to the state and to parents. Therefore, people should speak up and help each other to stop bullying.

Controversy Over Digital Art Increases

NINA YOUNG * *age 13*
Everett Middle School

Digital art is a relatively new art medium that has recently been blowing up in art communities worldwide. But like all things, it has its doubters. There are many artists, consumers, and critics who believe in traditional pen-on-paper format, and stand their ground in the opinion that digital is a form of "cheating" at art.

Amber T. Morelli, a prominent digital and traditional artist, begs to differ. "I think [people with this opinion] are very ignorant. How is it different from drawing on paper? You are still using your hands, and it's your drawing line for line...any digital artist who draws on the computer, for example, knows it takes a lot of time, we still mess up and we still have to start from scratch and end the drawing the same way," she says.

Many art critics from magazines known for art reviews such as *The New Yorker* sometimes argue that there are many features of digital art programs that make things easier, such as zoom features or layer tools. Most artists who use art programs like this, however, know that you must also develop skills to properly maneuver tools and the program itself.

Professional artist and exhibitioner, Rachel Beth Egenhoefer, offers a more neutral point of view. "I don't think digital art is easier, but art isn't really about that. Art is about the concept and the message, no matter how it's made. But digital art is still something you work hard at," she says.

Digital art isn't a lesser-known medium. Recently, an artist called David Hockney has been exhibiting not only traditional sceneries and concepts, but his art done on an iPad as well. Using a stylus and an app called "Brushes," Hockney is able to recreate images of lush abstract and greenery. His art is currently in exhibitions all over the world, and was recently shown at the de Young Museum here in San Francisco. Generally, digital art has received good reviews from the public, but it has its skeptics. "The world has become digital these days, so most things done digitally might be considered 'the easy way,' but the only difference is that it isn't drawn in pencil," concludes Morelli.

Soul Surfers

CATE REIKER * *age 9*
Ocean Shore School

In my neighborhood of Pedro Point there are a lot, and I mean a lot, of surfers. They are all kind of different. Some of them have surfed Mavericks, some of them just like to rip in Rockaway, and some are just "soul surfers." Right now we are just going to talk about soul surfers.

"Soul surfer" is a term coined in the 1960s to describe a surfer who surfs for the sheer pleasure of surfing. From the 1960s to the present, people still think soul surfing is like this.

I received a book called *365 Days of Wonder: Mr. Brown's Book of Precepts* written by my favorite author, R. J. Palacio. Precepts are "words to live by." I asked my neighbors and family friends who I feel are soul surfers to give their surfing words to live by.

Jeff Clark was the first surfer to find and surf Maverick waves. "If you can see yourself doing the impossible, then it's not impossible. If you can see yourself achieving your goals, then you have to see the work that you will have to put in to get there. If you commit yourself to it, you will achieve it." I agree with Jeff because if you think you can do something, you can.

Surfing also makes you calm. If you're feeling frustrated, you can go into the water and surf and it will calm you down. Dana Pifer, a breast cancer survivor who started surfing in

1981 says, "Surfing teaches us a form of meditation and to be patient. We don't get to decide, Mother Nature decides."

There are no titles in the water. Asi Ghiassi, who has been surfing since 1995, said, "Everybody is equal in the water. It doesn't matter if you're an emergency room doctor, artist, or a bum. In the water there are no titles." To be a soul surfer, you don't have to only surf all day. The only requirement is to love to surf.

My aunt Camille Keating started surfing in 1980 and is a true soul surfer. She lives on a boat dock and can see the ocean every day. "Each time you surf, your soul is somehow nourished. And there is no better way to fall asleep at night than by having a dose of Vitamin Sea," she said.

I think that surfing should just be for the fun of it. It's not about winning; it's about going out with your friends and getting barreled. My uncle, Tom Alexander, has been surfing since 1965 and he lives half the time in Maui, half the time here. He says, "surfing brings you closer to nature, and there is nothing better than surfing with a family member or friend."

For the Love of Diversity

ALEJANDRO COLINDRES * *age 14*
Mission High School

For as long as many people can remember, racism has lingered in society. For example, back in 2011, the school board in Arizona declared a statewide ban on all Ethnic Studies courses. The views of the board were based on false, racist accusations, primarily that the classes were only teaching students anti-American views.

Tom Horne, the Superintendent of Public Instruction, pushed the bill saying, "They divide [students] by race and teach each group about its own background only." This statement had no valid reasoning. Dividing students and teaching about a certain race's background is exactly what classes were doing before. The Latino community and any other minorities were excluded from the discussion. The school board, along with Tom Horne, had no real right to ban Ethnic Studies classes. On the contrary, Ethnic Studies has helped to encourage students of color and minority students through the use of ethnically relevant role models and materials.

In a recent interview, Ms. Riechel, an Ethnic Studies teacher, said that "for students, education without Ethnic Studies is less relevant. I support the expansion of Ethnic Studies."

According to a report from the National Education Association, "As students of color proceed through the school system, research finds that the overwhelming dominance of Euro-American perspectives leads many such students to disengage from academic learning."

On the other hand, studies that were done about middle school students taking Ethnic Studies documented high levels of student engagement, making a positive impact on student achievement and attitudes toward learning.

I believe that Ethnic Studies improves education by enriching curricula and improving student attitudes toward learning. My experience with Ethnic Studies has been a really fun and educational one. I've learned quite a lot about my culture, and my peers' cultures. Ethnic Studies shouldn't be banned. I think that Ethnic Studies should be offered more widely as a course. If it was discontinued, like it was in Arizona, then it should be brought back for the benefit of the students.

The Cartoon Adventures of Emma T Capps

JULIA REIKER ✳ *age 11*
Ocean Shore School

At age eleven, Emma T Capps came to 826 Valencia for a comic class. She is now applying to colleges, and she has had a big cartooning adventure along the way.

"I've been drawing since I could pick up a pencil," says Emma. After her 826 Valencia class she created a short comic known as *Tomorrow*. This new interest in cartooning didn't end, of course! She kept making cartoons and greeting cards. In eighth grade, Scholastic hosted a middle school and high school cartooning contest, where she won a medal for her cartoon called *Jam Days*.

The Chapel Chronicles, which Emma started at age fourteen, is a story about Chapel, a young spunky girl with fiery red hair who has intellectual adventures with her hedgehog, Rupert, loves hats, and has a brother named Barnaby. (In my opinion she is a bit of a dork, in a good way.) Emma created Chapel one night when she couldn't go to sleep, and this character somehow intrigued her. She kept on making tiny cartoons and greeting cards with her, and eventually made them into webcomics, which she has made every week for the last four years.

"Growing up I always wanted red hair, so Chapel inherited that," said Emma. She also says that Chapel is not based on herself — in fact, she says that Chapel can be more immature than she is. "But she definitely would be my friend if she was real." I understood when she said that all her characters "feel like my children in a way."

In July 2013, a special comic from *The Chapel Chronicles* was published in *Dark Horse Presents*, a major comics anthology — making her the only teenager published by Dark Horse. She has other cartoons on the side that will soon come to the world of books, like *Delays Expected*, a "short autobiographical romp." Emma says that she will soon wrap up *The Chapel Chronicles* and is excited to introduce her new comic books, which she has been writing for years.

Emma now hosts her own comic classes at 826 Valencia and is happy that she can inspire other children's lives by teaching them how to make comics.

"To spread my love of comics to these kids is really amazing to me, and the idea that this could come full circle and that one of my students could go on to become a cartoonist is pretty powerful."

I recommend the books and the comic classes to young crusaders who have a love for the nerdy cuteness in life. You can purchase the books on her website, chapelchronicles.com, and find out when her next comic classes are at 826valencia.org.

Starting School Later

ELIA GONZALEZ * *age 15*
Mission High School

According to the American Academy of Pediatrics, "Insufficient sleep in adolescents [is] an important public health issue that significantly affects their health and safety, as well as their academic success."

The article, "Time in Schools: How Does the U.S. Compare?" published by the Center for Public Education, states that "California requires 1,080 hours and Korea requires 1,020 hours of instruction at the high school level." Korean schools teach sixty hours less than U.S. schools and they still do better than us academically. Our school days are also longer than those in other countries. For example: "[An] average school day in Finland is five hours long" (According to the article "Finland's A+ Schools") compared to our U.S. average of eight hours, not including after-school programs.

One way to solve this problem could be by starting school later, taking away some hours or even taking out some school days. The main idea is to have fewer hours in school. That way we can have more time to rest and we can get more sleep, because it's not healthy for us to stay up late doing homework, playing sports, etc. and be forced to wake up early the next day for school. If we are not well-rested we are not going to be able to learn or focus in our classes and do well in school.

According to Ray from the Mission High School Wellness Center, "Teenagers need at least eight hours of sleep or more a night," but students are not getting that regularly. And according to a new report by the American Academy of Pediatrics that came out earlier this year: "Moving bedtimes earlier is not going to fix the problem, particularly for adolescents. Teens stay up later not because they don't want to go to sleep, but because they can't. Due to the delayed release of melatonin in the adolescent brain and a lack of sleep drive in response to fatigue, teens do not feel sleepy until much later at night than young children or adults, and have difficulty falling asleep, even when they are tired."

As I wrote before, schools in other countries have fewer hours of instruction than we do and they are doing better or the same as we are. We need more information on the benefits of starting school later to help people take this seriously. We also need more information on sleeping habits to help teenagers get better sleep. Teachers should also be better informed as to how assigning too much homework overworks us and causes us to not get enough sleep as well.

Dodgers and Giants

SONYA LEE * *age 13*
Everett Middle School

The cheering is equally loud for both teams at the Giants vs. Dodgers game at AT&T Park. The stadium is filled with orange and blue fans filling almost every seat. There is tension in the air as the two rival teams play the first game of the series.

The longtime rivalry between the Giants and the Dodgers started in the late 1800s. Both teams originally came from New York. The New York Giants and the Brooklyn Dodgers played each other frequently, causing tension which was how the rivalry was born. The rivalry peaked in the years 1946-1971, according to the book *The Giants and the Dodgers: Four Cities, Two Teams, One Rivalry.*

In the year 1957, the Major League Baseball officials told the Dodgers and the Giants that they could move to the West Coast, but only if they both agreed to move. In the end, both teams chose to move to the West Coast, making fans in California overjoyed while New Yorkers were heartbroken. Both teams moved to California, changing their names from the Brooklyn Dodgers and the New York Giants to the Los Angeles Dodgers and the San Francisco Giants.

According to the website dodger-giants.com, the Giants have had 1,210 head-to-head wins against the Dodgers while the Dodgers have had only 1,184. (They've tied seventeen times.) Having both teams in the same general area caused yet more tension because they played each other often.

Darryl Forman, a longtime sports fan and a resident of San Francisco, believes that the rivalry will never die out. In fact, she remembers when it was a three-way rivalry. The Yankees, the Dodgers, and the Giants were all rivals in New York. Forman remembers one particular game that she went to when the Dodgers and the Yankees were in the World Series. She said, "All the dads were wearing Dodgers gear and all the kids were wearing Yankees."

Divorce Is the Worst

ANDREA AYALA * *age 14*
Mission High School

I have seen many cases where my friends drastically change moods due to family issues. Divorce has some major effects on children, causing them to be depressed and isolated. Divorce is the effect of two parents not thinking thoroughly about their decision to get married in the first place, causing them to separate.

Miscommunication, intolerance, and arguing are often the things that lead parents to divorce. Kids are being left right in the middle of their parents' arguments, and are not always able to cope with the divorce. It leads to them consequently blaming themselves. In school, they are thinking too much about who they are going to be with and they get distracted. As days go by, they are left struggling with issues of parental custody, and then it affects their learning. When kids feel depressed, they tend to be lonely and not want to do anything.

"Healthy marriages are good for couples' mental and physical health. They are also good for children; growing up in a happy home protects children from mental, physical, educational, and social problems. However, about 40 to 50 percent of married couples in the United States divorce," says the American Psychological Association. When parents get divorced, all the positive aspects of marriage can get reversed.

The kids are the most affected. They face stress when being exposed to their parents' conflicts. How can we help these kids? Things that schools can do include trying to get some programs to help their students. I interviewed Olga Muñoz, a counselor at Mission High School's Wellness Center. The interview covered questions like: Have kids come to you for advice on divorce? How have you helped these children? And is it common? Muñoz is a social services worker, and she spoke about how she helps kids by giving them comfort and understanding their point of view. She also mentioned that it is a very common and sensitive issue. She believes that schools can help a lot by providing better support groups to help kids. She said, "I've seen a lot of students get really depressed over their problems at home," which tells us that this issue is practically everywhere and affecting everyone.

Most parents choose court as their "go-to" solution during a divorce, but I believe that's a bad idea. I think that putting the parents and children in counseling groups will help the situation. For example, there are health facilities that have developed a program called "Parenting Plan." It helps parents handle their future "parent-to-child" relationship. This group wants to minimize the effect of divorce on children. They wish to smooth the transition and make the changes easier, hoping the children won't fail later on. It is time to have schools help these children and help them thrive.

California's Report Card

VIVIAN REDMOND * *age 13*
Everett Middle School

California is a rich, diverse state with a wonderful past. But it is ranked forty-fifth in reading and math among other states in the U.S. How?

California has a couple of strong reasons for its struggles. One of them is that according to the Census Bureau, California has the highest poverty rate of any state by far. This means that many kids show up to school without supplies, without food to eat, and are too busy worrying about whether they will have a place to sleep at night to concentrate at school. Also, California has a very large population of non-English-speaking immigrants. Therefore, it is harder for English teachers to succeed.

Right now, California's standardized testing is going through a gigantic change. We used to have fill-in-the-bubble multiple choice questions called STAR Tests. Instead, we will have electronic Common Core tests that are supposed to be better. But are they? Education officials took a field test this spring to see how it would work and it showed great results. Our state has had two years, starting last year, to create amazing tests that will be great in the future.

But we can change our rank. According to Pam Slater, a public information officer who works in Sacramento, "Students themselves are the key to a great education—by helping their fellow students, their schools, and their communities."

So, help. Make sure you, your classmates, and friends are helping everyone get a better education.

"And while we are by no means out of the woods," Slater said, "we are on the right path."

What's that? You thought we only published works from our own programs? Heck no! Some of our favorites are from far off places, coming in via paper planes and carrier pigeons. We'll take stuff from any compelling writers world-wide (as long as they're between the ages of six and eighteen, that is!).

At-Large Submissions

Curls and Caps: Hope and Hip-Hop

JACKSON PLUT * *age 16*
Urban School, San Francisco, California

May I have your *attention please? May I have your attention please? Will the real Slim Shady please stand up?*

Light illuminates my phone. I push myself off the fluffy pillow, grab a comb, and start working on the curls, even though only five or six people will notice. Click. On. The music plays, the drums slowly building up as I open my blinds to the rising sun. A woman's voice. A black woman. Lauryn Hill. Smooth and jazzy. Nas's genius lyrics cut in. I'm rapping with him now, in the third and final verse. I'm pulling my comb through my hair. Combing for nobody. My feet are tapping. I finish the verse with Nas: *If I ruled the world.* What if I did? What would I change? I stop combing my curls. I accept they will never be perfect, so I smash a cap on top of them. I glance at the clock and bolt, stopping only to throw my headphones on to blast another song.

When I first embraced music I was four years old, a little black boy with curls. I was listening to my dad's records: Beatles, Stones, Marley, Rush, Nat King Cole, Steely Dan, and Otis Redding. Most of these artists are still on the favorites playlist in my ever-expanding musical library.

When I listened to music, I could imagine anything; without it, I could imagine nothing. I could be a superhero, in a place where people didn't tease me, where my family didn't get stares. I was immediately tied to music. I think about my naive self back then, when I didn't know what it meant to be black wishing that now I could go back to a time when I didn't have to look at the mirror and wonder why God gave me frizzy hair. I slip into a seat on the bus. Not a great way to start such a big day, thinking such dark thoughts—dark as my curly hair, tangling me within the terrorizing claws of race.

When I was little, my parents bought me a book about how to love my hair. A Negro's hair. The hair that suffered 300 years of oppression. The hair that survived it. All through grade school, the white kids wanted to touch my hair. For someone who had never seen a black person before, it was like going rug shopping for the first time. Or maybe more like petting an animal for the first time. I was never as fascinated with white people's hair. But all my friends used to stare at mine and say, *I love touching it so much*, but that was when we were kids –not that it's changed. Yet another reason to smash a cap over my head, to protect myself from the predators. White claws preying on my hair, my traditions, my hard work. I didn't know how to make them stop, I still don't.

Now I've arrived at a big school event at the Herbst Theater in San Francisco; I listen as the tech people instruct students, "Set this up! Set that up!" I feel some butterflies in my stomach, so I start thinking about things to make me feel better. Otis Redding and Sam Cooke. That's good music, good hair. Curls like the weeds at the bottom of the muddy Mississippi but also at the bottom of the Nile. My hair is and always will be my roots, maybe going back to the smallest town in the smallest county in Burkina Faso. Once I didn't understand the roots of the music I loved. I hated jazz when I was young, but that changed once I started to study the history, my history. I think of Immortal Technique, a political activist with a tongue of fire. I hate it when they tell us how far we've come to be; as if our people's history started with slavery. The good and the bad, they were my people, with my skin, my hair. Through music I discovered more and more about myself: as a learner, as a man, as an African American.

I go to the theater bathroom and change, running my pick through my hair. I pull out the whole setup: Vaseline, cocoa butter, spray. Not that anyone will notice.

Once I realized that music was a good road to travel on, I began to sprint down the path at full speed. In seventh grade, I joined a world music group that performed in Salzburg, Austria. We practiced. We danced. We played. And music, slowly, steadily, came toward me. When we finally met, it embraced me. It was as if we were long lost friends. I remember stepping on stage, performing our body music, smiling, hair glowing after hours of combing. I remember playing a Vivaldi tune on the xylophone, a jazz tune on the vibes, and break dancing to a fusion of jazz and hip-hop. I remember stepping to the front of the stage and performing a six step in front of hundreds of Europeans unfamiliar with break dancing and hip-hop culture. I tried my hardest to play every note with passion, with love and with care.

The Herbst Theater is filling up. I pull up my pants and do up my belt. I pat my hair, looking in the mirror. Still doesn't look perfect. I grab the comb.

Dave, my barber, would laugh if he saw me trying to comb out my hair with pants on and no shirt, frantic to do an hour-long process in five minutes. My barbershop, Chicago's, is in the heart of the Fillmore in San Francisco. It is a traditional black barbershop, but has barbers of all races working there. I have been going to Chicago's to get my hair done since I was a little kid. If I told anyone from school I had to get a haircut, they would say, "Your hair's not long" or "You don't need a haircut, stupid," and stroke their perfect long and straight hair. The fact was, I did need a haircut, or my line would go out of place and my hair wouldn't be straight. I have to maintain my hair, even if no one else cares. I sit in the shop and listen to the barbers discuss music: funk, jazz, soul, and my favorite: old-school hip-hop. I watch my cut hair fall from my head, like drops from a fountain, as I hear them say, "*Illmatic* was a much better album," and play "Try a Little Tenderness." I finish combing and put on my shirt. I open the bathroom door and walk slowly down the hallway to the big doors at the end. I pass those up and keep walking to our small room at the side of the stage where we all wait.

How good it felt to be part of Chicago's community, an African American community. I grab my mallets and walk back stage. The group before us is just finishing up; wailing saxophone and steady drum rhythms carry them. I hear hands clapping, matching the music. I get nervous so, again, I comb my hair and put on a little more cocoa butter. We're on, I hear from behind the curtain. I glance at myself in the mirror. Not perfect, but good. Good enough to make me proud. I step on stage to applause, then silence, followed by the crash of symbols. Then I begin to play. I quickly become lost in the rhythm, but not trapped, just guided along by it. I look and see faces staring at me, at my uncovered hair. I am showing my roots, my tradition. I have put myself out on this stage, and I feel accepted by the world and comforted by the music. I feel the warm stares of my parents in the audience. This morning I was singing alone at home in my room as I combed my hair, pulling the comb through the tangles of my insecurity. I put my lips forward to the mic and sing with the rest of the band. Happiness comes to me on stage and makes me glow. The glow starts at my feet, goes slowly up to my stomach, to my neck, and finally reaches my hair, nicely combed and gleaming in the lights. I am confident, proud of my hair. I feel my roots, my tradition, myself surging through each note I play. All I need is one mic.

Swim Your Heart Out

NICHOLAS ROSSO * *age 15*
Westfield High School, Westfield, Massachusetts

It was pep talk—the time when my coach, Tom, told my team and me what we were going to swim. We were all anxious; this was our biggest meet of the year against our rivals, Minnechaug. I was sitting on the bleachers twiddling my thumbs as my coach read the first event.

He said, "The people swimming in the 200 IM are Tim, Gabe, and Nick." Personally, I did not want to do that, but I had no say. I didn't pay attention in the second event because I knew I wasn't going to be in that, and then he started the third event. "Slav and Nick," Tom turned to me, "Now Nick, I discussed this decision with Jimmy and he thought it would be a good idea because we need him for the 100 breast so he can beat Tommy, but you also need to beat who you're racing even if it's Tommy."

I replied, "Okay, but how do you want me to swim it?"

"By swimming your heart out," he said. The pressure was set on me; I needed to win that race.

It was the day of the meet. We were all on the bus, and of course, me being the way I am, I started to panic. My friend Reiley was sitting next to me; she has a calming demeanor. I kept ranting about how I was only a freshman and Tommy was a senior and this race would be so bad and that I wouldn't be able to win. Reiley calmed me down and helped encourage me to pump me up for the race. During warm ups, all I could think about was that race.

I was thinking *What if I don't win? Will Jimmy be mad at me? Will everyone be mad at me? But what if I win? Will Tommy hate me? Not that I even care if he does, but will they try to disqualify me in some way?* I was going crazy and just wanted to get the race over with.

Finally, it came time for me to swim that dreaded race. Walking up to the block all I could hear was the murmur of the crowd. The smell of chlorine filled my lungs. I looked to my left and saw the Minnechaug team dressed in blue. Looking to my right, I saw red and black, my colors, the ones that reminded me that I had support for this race. A couple of my friends wished me good luck from the other end of the pool. I was behind the block stretching when Tommy came up to me and gave a hand shake and wished me good luck. Now, there was not much of a difference between Tommy and me, we were both about equal height—around five feet ten inches— with an athletic build. My heart started to race, just like I was going to have to do. The whistle blows, we step up, and time stops. I started to panic deep inside, but I needed to suppress that and focus on the task at hand. BEAT TOMMY!

The starter's voice said, "Take your mark." I bent down and gripped the block and made my knuckles turn white. Then, "BEEP!" I shoved off the block and slipped through the water as I entered the pool. As I was kicking under water, I saw out of the corner of my eye that Tommy started to get a lead on me; I kicked harder. Coming up for my first breath was refreshing; I got my strength back to catch up to him. We were closing in on our flip turn. The wall came and I turned as fast as my body would let me no matter how much pain there was. I pushed off that wall like a torpedo.

This was it, the last lap; I had to give it all or nothing. When I came to the surface and took my first breath, I saw my team and all the parents from my team screaming at the edge of the pool and flailing their arms. The sight of Tommy next to me couldn't be seen because I was making so much white water, so I had no idea if he was ahead, behind, or right next to me. I did not care; I kicked and moved my hands as fast as I could. The wall was getting closer and closer, just a few more strokes. With a powerful force, the tips of my fingers made contact to the touchpads.

Lifting my head out of the water, I heard roaring, but it wasn't coming from the side that I wanted it to. I looked at the clock and saw why I didn't win. Tommy beat me by .12 seconds. The difference was the size of a fingernail. I was so disappointed with myself. Tommy and I shook hands and we got out of the water and parted our separate ways. When I got back to my team, they all came up to me and told me "good job" and all the phrases that are supposed to be said. I went straight to my coach to talk to him about it.

All he said was "That was a good race, and you shouldn't be disappointed that you lost because that was close, and you are only a freshman, almost beating a senior. You have potential, and I want to work with you next season to improve your strokes and make you faster, so next year you'll blow the competition out of the water. Hell, there won't even be any competition for you because you'll be so fast! Now go sit and rest."

When I started to ascend up the bleachers, my friends flooded around me. They all told me "good job" and said that I shouldn't let the loss get to me, but I did. I was depressed for the rest of the meet. I kept wondering what I did wrong. I figured it out that it was my start; I was too slow. I did not let my depression get to me in my other races that meet; I prospered in those. The meet finally came to an end, filled with blood pressure-rising races, including my own, which I was thankful for. We lost two races and one of them was mine. I kept beating myself up for losing, telling myself that if I did win then maybe we could have lost by less or maybe we could have won because it could have inspired Jimmy, who lost the other race, to win. On the bus ride home, I got my mind off things and was singing songs with my friends at the top of my lungs. Now I do not even care about that race anymore. What happened in the past stays in the past. I have moved on and trained harder and I will be able to win all of my races this year.

Generalized State

SKYLER LACEY * *age 14*
Vacaville High School, Vacaville, California

You don't understand.

You're there, while I'm here.

California kids—adults even—glorified by makeup and movie sets. Depicted to be rich enough to have dollars and coins to set the path to self-destruction. Thought to live so close to the beach, they sit outside in the morning to see a sunrise reflecting off of the sea like a mirror.

California is a place where celebrities walk down the street like a meet and greet.

Generalizations have always bothered me, especially kinds like this.

California isn't a dream.

Girls aren't orange poppies waiting to be picked by plaid shorts and a pastel polo shirt with a smile whiter than the bones that threaten to puncture their skin.

There's always more to a picture than a black and white filter with a sad quote and fancy font slapped on it. Nobody thinks about what's behind it.

Shops and vendors scattered around Venice Beach; the actual pain in the eyes of those behind the camera who have to face their harsh reality every day.

By "perfect weather," do you mean 100 degree heat in the fall when it's rain's time to shine?

Before you jump in the pool, remember that we're in a drought.

Growing up in such disorder, where everything is manipulated to the extent that it's where every soul yearns to be. If you live here, you'd know that we call it normalcy.

Come to California—promise me your dreams won't disappoint you. Try to look past the pollution in the water. Come to stare at the girls with shorts short enough to keep your imagination running amuck, along with the brightly colored Hollister sweaters to cover up the brutality of California perfection.

What is California, you ask?

California is the dream.

God's Calling

WILLIAM ZENG * *age 17*
Lowell High School, San Francisco, California

My sister was married on a Sunday in a modest, off-white, two story church building. Normally it was run by Lutherans, but every Sunday the church building was rented to a church of Chinese Christians, who in turn rented it to my family for a day.

The day started off with service, where about fifty late-in-life first generation Chinese Americans made their way into the cushioned wooden pews. Then, with great gusto, an organ was played, indicating the start of mass. From the hidden entrances on the sides of the room, members of the choir, wearing wine-colored robes, slowly walked up to the stage. If I had committed to the church, I could've been in one of those robes. They sang their song and requested that we stand up to sing along. Thus began the draining process of listening to Chinese men and women, all of grandchild-having age and older, singing songs in Chinese praising a white Jesus.

The choir was eventually replaced by Pastor Tien and his translator, who relayed everything Pastor Tien said from Mandarin to Cantonese. I had tried to follow along, but my Chinese, in both dialects, was inept at best. Also I was busy comparing Quentin Tarantino's version of Ezekiel 25:17 to that of the Bible. I liked the movies better.

Between the service and the wedding, there was a gap for everybody who wasn't there for the wedding to leave, and for everybody who was to enter. I stood outside for a moment. Looking at the church building from the outside, I realized this was the first time in years since I had been in church. I used to go to church every Sunday. I was baptized at the church. I used to celebrate Easter, Thanksgiving, and Christmas at the church. I wondered to myself, how I had drifted so far from something that used to be so close.

I find it hard to believe anyone who has told me about a sudden and major shift in their life. For me, things have always been a gradual change, like that of day to night. The sun doesn't just disappear out of sight. It inches through and eventually out of the sky within the span of an entire day. My departure from the church was like that–the sun setting. It was easier to stay home than sit through two hours of being constantly reminded of how linguistically disconnected I was from my culture. Ironically enough, it was this fear of shame from not knowing fluent Chinese that drove me away from learning Chinese. I wasn't really convinced about God either. For me, the idea of an omnipotent and benevolent force creating the entire world was riddled with logical potholes.

However, in retrospect, I wish I had stuck with them. I wish I still had a place I could call my own, that I was more involved in my culture, that I could still be a part of this community, despite all of its contradictions. I didn't care if the churchgoers had read the Bible or not, if they believed in God or not, that their version of Ezekiel 25:17 was decidedly more boring than Quentin Tarantino's, or that they praised white Jesus, a product of Eurocentrism. I just wanted to realign myself with my past.

After the ceremony, there was a wedding dinner. We said our prayers and started serving food. After all the food was passed out, I ended up sitting on a couch opposite Pastor Tien. Pastor Tien was a tall and lanky man in his mid-seventies with dark and wrinkled skin, like a water chestnut. He remembered my name. He always did. At first I tried talking to him in Mandarin, when he, realizing how little I could speak, started talking in English. We started making small talk and the conversation led itself to his career as a holy man. In his early twenties, Pastor Tien decided that God's calling was for him to become a pastor. Thus he studied theology in what at the time was the British colony of Hong Kong, and started teaching the word of God.

It astounded me to think that someone could be so passionate about something, especially something as abstract and unknowable as God, and have it guide a majority of their adult life. I couldn't imagine committing myself to anything the way Pastor Tien did to his faith. I wanted to, though, imagine myself feeling that way.

There was a pause, and just as I thought our conversation had ended, he turned to me and said, "I hope you find God's calling for you." We had that in common.

Even though I didn't believe in God, or at least not in a God or gods that any church touted, hearing Pastor Tien say that was one of the most comforting things I had felt. For so long, I was led to believe that I was solely responsible for my own life, that I had to take charge and forge my own path. I imagined that every success was mine and every failure crushing. And here was this sage-like figure telling me it was not so. Perhaps it is fanciful to imagine that our lives are dictated by an omnipresent force, but I find it supremely vain to imagine ourselves as the single architect of our lives.

It Can Be Gone that Fast

SEAN BENNETT * *age 13*
Madison Junior School, Madison, New Jersey

BANG!

"Sean!" screamed my Little League baseball coach, "You're on deck!" The sound of a bat being violently hit against a metal fence woke me from my day dream.

"Huh?" I mumbled.

"You're batting up next," whispered a boy sitting next to me.

It was late July, and I was eight years old. I had just moved to Madison in the beginning of the year, and I was grateful for how nice everyone was to me, but at the same time I missed my old friends from White Meadow Lake.

While I was waiting to get up to bat, I saw my neighbor's car pull into the driveway next to the field. Confused and impatient, I tried to make the person who was batting hurry up because I thought my neighbor was here to pick me up. She ran up to the field quickly, I was wondering why she was in such a hurry, so I tried to talk to her but she just ran up to me ignoring what I was saying. Surprisingly, she was in tears while she told me my house was on fire. At first I was too stunned to actually have any reaction at all, but she told me to come into her car.

On the way to my house I was thinking to myself, it's probably not that bad, maybe the oven burned something or a candle fell over and started a small fire. You wouldn't believe how wrong I was.

As Mrs. Dines, my neighbor, drove me toward my house, I saw the smoke and thought, *this is much worse than I expected.* This is when everything went blank for me. I had no expression, no emotion, and no thoughts. I just sat in the backseat of the car and stared at the smoke.

Then it came into view.

The top half of my house was engulfed in flames. Firemen were spraying water all over the fire, but it was too overpowering. As I was watching the top half of my house being overwhelmed by a huge inferno, a thought popped into my head. Bailey. My eleven-year-old dog was home when the fire happened. I looked to my left and my right, but she was nowhere to be seen. I started panicking and asking the firemen where my dog was, and they all just said that they were trying to find her and that they would do their best. The feeling of the scorching heat on my face, the smell of smoke and the brackish taste of my own tears was all too much for me, and I just waited. I waited for all of it to be over. Looking straight at the fire, hoping it would stop, for almost an hour.

Finally, I saw my dog emerge from the smoky scene and she ran up to me. I was overjoyed to see her okay and know that everyone was safe.

After the fire, my life was never the same. I had finally appreciated how generous everyone was in Madison. The church and school I went to had both raised money for my family, without us even asking. The school had even set up a program where other families provided us with dinners because we were living in a hotel for seven weeks. All the people who had donated money were like heroes to me at that time in my life. I am still amazed that people I had never even met before were giving away money and food to my family and me.

My family and I moved into a house just down the street from the destroyed house, so we could check on how the reconstruction was going. I was still having trouble with loss, because everything I had ever had was gone. With no warning, out of nowhere—everything, gone. This whole experience made me learn a very important life lesson. And that is never take anything for granted, because it can disappear in the blink of an eye, because when it's gone, you're unquestionably going to miss it.

You made it! You're probably thinking, "Phew! Now I know every single thing that happens at 826 Valencia. There's nothing more to know." And that's where you're wrong. There are more people and projects involved in a single week at 826 than we could fit in this entire book. Just imagine that for every name, publication, and program listed in the coming pages, there are a few hundred names of volunteers, too. This may sound fantastic, but you just finished reading *the 826 Quarterly*. Your imagination should be pretty limbered up by now.

826 Valencia

Who We Are & What We Do

The People of 826 Valencia

STAFF

Bita Nazarian *Executive Director*
Allyson Halpern *Development Director*
Amy Popovich *Production Coordinator*
Ashley Varady *Programs Manager*
Caroline Kangas *Pirate Store Manager*
Christina V. Perry *Programs Director*
Claudia Sanchez *Programs Coordinator*
Emma Peoples *Programs Assistant*
Jorge Eduardo Garcia *Programs Director*
Lauren Hall *Grants and Evaluations Director*
María Inés Montes *Design Director*
Molly Parent *Programs Manager*
Olivia White Lopez *Volunteer Engagement Manager*

**AMERICORPS SUPPORT STAFF
THROUGH SUMMER 2015**

Alyssa Aninag *Volunteer Engagement Assistant*
Amanda Loo *Development Assistant*
Desta Lissanu *Programs Assistant*
Pablo Baeza *Programs Assistant*

THE BELOVED INTERNS OF 826 VALENCIA

SUMMER 2014

Alexandra Cotrim	Julianna Ponce
Analee Lapreziosa	Lauren Boranian
Angelina Brand	Maggie Kaprosch
Angeline Rodriguez	Olivia Buntaine
Blair Meehan	Pearl Khuu
Chris Yang	Sarah Andrews
Claudia Waldman	Sarah Macklis
Daisy Guzman	Sergio Gomez
Ellen Waddell	Tamara Tanujaya
Glyn Peterson	Tracy Liu
Hannah Schiff	Trevor Mattingly
Henna Rahimi	

FALL 2014

Adriana del Mar	Jan Chen
Diana Martin	Katy Jensen
Dominique Santos	Katya Bitar
Eric Pang	Laurel Fujii
Erika Ramos	Marty Oropeza
Fiona Warrington	Sandy Tsai
Hannah Lassiter	Tracy Liu

THE 826 VALENCIA BOARD OF DIRECTORS

Andrew Strickman	Joya Banerjee
Barb Bersche	Matt Middlebrook
Dave Pell	Meg Ray
Eric Abrams	Michael Beckwith
Jim Lesser	Vendela Vida

826 VALENCIA CO-FOUNDERS
Nínive Calegari and Dave Eggers

OUR VOLUNTEERS
There's absolutely no way we could create hundreds of publications and serve thousands of students annually without a legion of volunteers. These incredible people work in all realms, from tutoring to fundraising and beyond. They range in age, background and expertise but all have a shared passion for our work with young people. Volunteers past and present, you know who you are. Thank you, thank you, thank you.

826 NATIONAL
826 Valencia's success has spread across the country. Under the umbrella of 826 National, writing and tutoring centers have opened up in seven more cities. If you would like to learn more about other 826 programs, please visit the following websites.

826 National	**826 DC**	**826 NYC**
826national.org	826dc.org	826nyc.org
826 Boston	**826 LA**	**826 Valencia**
826boston.org	826la.org	826valencia.org
826 CHI	**826 Michigan**	
826chi.org	826michigan.org	

Our Programs

We are so proud of the student writing collected in this, the twenty-first edition of *the 826 Quarterly*. It is the result of countless hours of hard work by students and teachers alike. We are also endlessly inspired by our hardworking tutors, all of whom make the following programs possible. If you have not yet visited 826 Valencia, or if it has been a while, please do come by to see us — we'll treat you to a good mopping, free of charge.

The work collected in this edition of *the 826 Quarterly* came from the following programs:

AFTER-SCHOOL TUTORING

During the school year, 826 Valencia is packed five days a week with neighborhood students who come in after school for free one-on-one tutoring in all subject areas. During the 2013-2014 school year, we expanded our after-school tutoring program with a twice-weekly evening session geared toward the unique needs of older students in grades seven through twelve. Students of all ages also have access to Sunday drop-in tutoring. During the summer, these students participate in our five-week Exploring Words Summer Camp, where we explore the STEM curriculum (Science, Technology, Engineering, and Math) in addition to our traditional creative writing focus through projects and writing prompts in a super fun environment.

IN-SCHOOLS

We dispatch teams of volunteers into local high-need schools around the city to support teachers and provide one-on-one assistance to students as they tackle various projects, including school newspapers, research papers, oral histories, and college entrance essays. We give additional support to nearby Everett Middle and Mission High Schools, where we staff two dedicated 826 Writers' Rooms to support the teachers and students onsite throughout the year. We also have a satellite after-school program for third-, fourth-, and fifth-graders at Buena Vista Horace Mann, a bilingual K–8 school in the Mission District, in which English Language Learners work on creative writing to build their skills.

WORKSHOPS

826 Valencia offers free workshops designed to foster creativity and strengthen writing skills in a wide variety of areas, like cartooning, college entrance essay writing, or starting a 'zine. All workshops, from the playful to the practical, are project-based and are taught by experienced, accomplished professionals. Over the summer, our Young Authors' Workshop provides an intensive writing experience for high school-aged students over the course of two weeks.

We also offer the following core services, which keep our Writing Lab buzzing around the clock:

FIELD TRIPS

Up to four times a week, 826 Valencia welcomes an entire class for a morning of wacky high-energy learning. Our most popular field trip is one in which students write their own books and take home a bound copy complete with professional illustrations, all within a two-hour period.

COLLEGE AND CAREER READINESS

Each year, we offer a roster of programs designed to help students get to college and be successful there. We provide

six $15,000 scholarships to graduating seniors for their
college education, and serve 200 high school students annually via the Great San Francisco Personal Statement Weekend,
where students receive undivided attention on their college-
entrance essays. We also partner with ScholarMatch to offer
college-access workshops for our seventh- to twelfth-graders
during evening tutoring, which includes support as students
choose a college, apply for financial aid, and get on the path
to career readiness. ScholarMatch also provides ongoing
support to our scholarship winners while they are enrolled
in college to help them transition successfully.

PUBLISHING

Students in all of 826's programs have the ability to experience, appreciate, and create great writing in part because
of our professional-quality publishing. In addition to *the
826 Quarterly*, 826 Valencia publishes newspapers, magazines, books, chapbooks, and blogs — all created by students.
Experienced editors and designers are involved in these
projects to give students greater insight into the realities of
professional publishing. Our student books are publicized
through our website, community events, and the local media,
and some are sold nationwide.

TEACHER OF THE MONTH

From the beginning, part of 826 Valencia's goal has been to
support teachers. There are so many students who have had
their minds set aglow by a teacher's own zest for life and
learning, and we'd like to play a very small part in reward-
ing them. Teachers are nominated by students, parents, and
others who send in letters, pictures, and videos letting us
know how special the teacher is. Every month we hear about
so many amazing teachers, and we've been moved to tears
more than once. The monthly winner receives a check for
$1,500. Know a teacher you want to nominate? Guidelines
can be found at 826valencia.org. Submissions are due on the
15th of each month.

The Pirate Supply Store

"Definitely one of the top five pirate stores
I've been to recently." — DAVID BYRNE

What happens in the store at 826 Valencia? Many have said that upon entering San Francisco's only independent pirate-supply store, they get a sensation of déjà vu. Others walk in and feel at once the miracle work of an unseen hand. And there are those whose eyes bulge and shrink simultaneously, their thoughts so convoluted that they are unable to shout or mutter the question that most plagues them: "What is this place?"

PIRATE STORE STAFF & VOLUNTEERS

Staff	Recent Guest Artists
Chris Gomez	Lisa Congdon
Christian Hasselberger	Mathew Fleming
Caroline Kangas	Subject-Object
Byron Weiss	Kehau Lyons
Trevor Mattingly	Reina Takahashi
	Betabrand
	Shannon Weber

GIANT SQUID ACQUITTED OF
SHIPWRECKING CHARGES
By Rot-Thumbed Samuel

In a shocking turn of events fit for daytime melodrama, Zigfried the giant squid, who was charged last month with premeditated shipwrecking of the privateer vessel Incoherent Rambler, was acquitted of all charges thanks to the surprise testimony of his estranged twin brother, Gaillard. Gaillard confessed to the court that he used a large fake mustache to impersonate his brother during the shipwrecking. When questioned about his motive, Gaillard remorsefully expressed that his actions were purely spiteful and intended to get back at Zigfried for not planning a joint birthday party with him as they had done in previous years.

However, before Gaillard could be booked on charges of his own, the court was double-shocked to discover that neither squid was in fact responsible for the shipwreck, which was actually caused by a sea storm accidentally willed into being by the ghost of the squid brothers' childhood intramural cricket coach. We don't know if maritime law covers this kind of thing, but we'll keep you updated.

USELESS KNOTS THAT NEED TO BE RETIRED
BECAUSE I HATE THEM
By Gray Bones Mary

Every day we walk a balancing act between progress and tradition in this line of work. Sometimes, though, you need to take a stand for what makes the most sense and do away with old practices that are getting in the way. I know for a fact that knots are a place where we could all stand to clean house. Or clean ship. I actually did sail on a house once and it was a deeply enriching experience.

No matter what you might be sailing on, you have to hear me out, guys; some of these knots simply must go. The Half-Divine Trident Knot, for instance, is prone to jamming, and usually elicits a C&D letter from Poseidon on the grounds of intellectual property theft. I thought we were plundering for personal wealth and glory, not constant legal fees. Similarly, I would be thoroughly pleased if I never had to tie a Bronzed Zeppelin Hitch because, I'll be honest, it just reminds me of having to socialize with smug air ship captains at port towns. It also gets soggy really fast.

I'm not saying we need to throw the doubloons out with the cursed strongbox, but it is time to be honest about what's getting in the way of a successful voyage. Yes, there's a poetry to the loops of a Wayman's Grief Knot, or the artful bends of a Wayman's Emotional Healing Knot, but their usefulness has passed. Unless the reason we keep these old knots around is because if we don't, the ghosts of their original inventors will haunt us all. Nobody's told me if that's what's actually going on, but it seems likely.

OBITUARY-ESQUE OCCURANCES
By Probably-Cursed Philip

We've got this counter below deck for every time our boatswain Mickey thinks he's seen a ghost, a specter, a phantasm, or some such thing. It's quite nicely made, especially for a placard that we carved when we were bored, but I've always thought it needed more "5" cards because they seem to keep disappearing.

It had been some time since he'd claimed to encounter such a thing "while in a wistful moment of low spirits and standing on deck to contemplate the stars," as his stories nearly always start. But ever since we ran aground at Baffin Island, he's been hanging out with poltergeists constantly, and he never eats with the rest of the crew anymore. It's really starting to affect morale. Sure we had a few deep belly laughs when we got to bump up the numbers on the "Mickey's Banshee Extravaganza" counter, but it started to lose its charm when we ran out of fives. Seriously, what happened to the fives?

I did actually get a chance to talk to him this morning, though. He said that most of the ghosts think we should all get out of here because this island is practically in the Arctic and it's only getting colder, but we shouldn't worry about him because one of the ghosts had an extra pair of socks. And that he'd get back to us next month. May fortune favor your boldness in the face of the paranormal, Mickey, Bravest of Boatswains.

Other Books from 826 Valencia

826 Valencia produces a variety of publications, each of which contains work written by students in our various programs. Some are professionally printed and nationally distributed; others are glued together here and sold in the Pirate Supply Store. These projects represent some of the most exciting work at 826 Valencia, as they enable Bay Area students to experience a world of publishing not otherwise available to them. Visit 826valencia.org/store or your local bookstore to purchase the following publications:

 *Uncharted Places: An Atlas of Being Here* (2014) This collection of essays by fifty-two juniors and seniors at Thurgood Marshall High School examines the idea of "place" and what it means to these young authors. It contains stories about locales real and imagined, internal and external, places of transition and those of comfort. These young writers bravely share their views of the world, giving us a glimpse into the places that are most important to them—those not necessarily found on a map, but in the heart.

 *The Enter Question* (2013) is a collection of essays on issues of immigrant identity recounted in eighty-one distinct voices from the eleventh grade class at San Francisco International High School. The collection covers a wide variety of topics including the challenges of communicating in a new language, the courage it takes to ask for help, and the joy found in meeting new people from all over the world, in addition to challenges all teenagers face as they struggle to forge identity and community.

 *Arrive, Breathe, and Be Still* (2012) is a collection of monologues and plays exploring the themes of resistance and resilience written by thirty-five students at Downtown High School in San Francisco, with a foreword by playwright Octavio Solis. After a semester of working intensely with actors at the American Conservatory Theater and writing tutors from 826 Valencia, the students produced this powerful look into the realities of high school life, the pressures surrounding young people, and the strength it takes to keep going. Perfect for reading or performing, these pieces are a refreshing tool for using theater both in the classroom and outside of it.

 *Beyond Stolen Flames, Forbidden Fruit, and Telephone Booths* (2011) is a collection of essays and short stories, written by fifty-three juniors and seniors at June Jordan School for Equity, in which young writers explore the role of myth in our world today. Students wrote pieces of fiction and nonfiction, retelling old myths, creating new ones, celebrating everyday heroes, and recognizing the tales that their families have told over and over. With a foreword by Khaled Hosseini, the result is a collection with a powerful message about the stories that have shaped students' perspectives and the world they know.

A Time to Eat Cake (2011) is a collection of short pieces from the students in 826 Valencia's After-School Tutoring program. In collaboration with the San Francisco pastry shop Miette, students spent a month exploring memories, imagining their ideal treats, and spinning amazing tales of cake adventures. With a foreword by Miette founder Meg Ray, this book shows that you don't have to be Proust to know the power of sweets.

We the Dreamers (2010) is a collection of essays by fifty-one juniors at John O'Connell High School reflecting on what the American Dream means to them. The students recount stories about family, home, immigration, hardship, and the hopes of their generation—as well as those of the generation that raised them. The result is a firsthand account of these essayists' often-complicated relationship with our national ethos that is insightful, impassioned, surprising, and of utmost importance to our understanding of what the American Dream means for their generation.

Show of Hands (2009) is a collection of stories and essays written by fifty-four juniors and seniors at Mission High School. It amplifies the students' voices as they reflect on one of humanity's most revered guides for moral behavior: the Golden Rule, which tells us that we should act toward others as we would want them to act toward us. Whether speaking about global issues, street violence, or the way to behave among friends and family, the voices of these young essayists are brilliant, thoughtful, and, most of all, urgent.

Thanks and Have Fun Running the Country (2009) is a collection of letters penned by our After-School Tutoring students to newly -elected President Obama. In this collection, which arrived at inauguration time, there's loads of advice for the president, often hilarious, sometimes heartfelt, and occasionally downright practical. The letters have been featured in *The New York Times*, the *San Francisco Chronicle*, and on *This American Life*.

Seeing Through the Fog (2008) is a guidebook written by seniors from Gateway High School that explores San Francisco from tourist, local, and personal perspectives. Both whimsical and factually accurate, the pieces in this collection take the reader to the places that teenagers know best, from taquerias to skate spots to fashionable shops that won't break your budget.

Exactly (2007) is a hardbound book of colorful stories for children ages nine to eleven. This collection of fifty-six narratives by students at Raoul Wallenberg Traditional High School is illustrated by forty-three professional artists. It passes on lessons that teenagers want the next generation to know.

Inspired by magical realism, students at Galileo Academy of Science and Technology produced *Home Wasn't Built in a Day* (2006), a collection of short stories based on family myths and legends. With a foreword by actor and comedian Robin Williams, the book comes alive through powerful student voices that explore just what it is that makes a house a home.

I Might Get Somewhere: Oral Histories of Immigration and Migration (2005) exhibits an array of student-recorded oral narratives about moving to San Francisco from other parts of the United States and all over the world. Acclaimed author Amy Tan wrote the foreword to this compelling collection of personal stories by Balboa High School students. All these narratives shed light on the problems and pleasures of finding one's life in new surroundings.

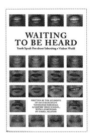
Written by thirty-nine students at Thurgood Marshall Academic High School, *Waiting to Be Heard: Youth Speak Out About Inheriting a Violent World* (2004) addresses violence and peace on a personal, local, and global scale. With a foreword by Isabel Allende, the book combines essays, fiction, poetry, and experimental writing to create a passionate collection of student expression.

Talking Back: What Students Know About Teaching (2003) is a book that delivers the voices of the class of 2004 from Leadership High School. In reading the book—previously a required-reading textbook at San Francisco State University and Mills College—you will understand the relationships students want with their teachers, how students view classroom life, and how the world affects students.

826 Valencia also publishes scores of chapbooks each semester. These collections of writing primarily come from two sources: our volunteer-taught evening and weekend workshops, and our in-school projects, where students work closely with tutors to edit their writing. Designed and printed right at 826 Valencia, the resulting chapbooks range from student-penned screenplays to collections of bilingual poetry.

PUBLICATIONS FOR STUDENTS & TEACHERS

 *Don't Forget to Write* (2005) contains fifty-four of the best lesson plans used in workshops taught at 826 Valencia, 826NYC, and 826LA, giving away all of our secrets for making writing fun. Each lesson plan was written by its original workshop teacher, including Jonathan Ames, Aimee Bender, Dave Eggers, Erika Lopez, Julie Orringer, Jon Scieszka, Sarah Vowell, and many others. If you are a parent or a teacher, this book is meant to make your life easier, as it contains enthralling and effective ideas to get your students writing. It can also be used as a resource for the aspiring writer. In 2011, 826 National published a two-volume second edition of *Don't Forget to Write*, also available in our Pirate Supply Store.

It's Always a Good Time to Give

WE NEED YOUR HELP

We could not do what we do without the thousands (yes, thousands) of volunteers who make our programs possible. We are always on the lookout for more volunteer tutors, and we also always need volunteers with software skills, advanced editing skills, and advanced design, illustration, and photography skills. If you've got a skill, we need your help. It's easy to become a volunteer and a bunch of fun to actually do it. Please fill out our online application to let us know you'd like to lend your time: **826valencia.org/volunteer.**

OTHER WAYS TO GIVE

Whether it's loose change or heaps of cash, a donation of any size will help 826 Valencia continue to offer a variety of free literacy and publishing programs to Bay Area youth. We would greatly appreciate your financial support.

Please make a donation at:
826valencia.org/donate

You can also mail your contribution to:
826 Valencia Street, San Francisco, CA 94110

Your donation is tax-deductible. What a plus! Thank you!